B.J. Was As Nervous As She'd Been The First Time She And Cairn Had Been Alone Like This....

She could still remember the sparkle of the lights on the water and the scent of cherry blossoms in the air as he'd pulled her ever so gently into his arms.

Lightning had flashed then, illuminating the demand in his dark eyes, and she could still feel the shivery excitement that had run over her.

Watching him now, she realized just how naive she'd been to think she could actually take a wild hawk, confine him to a cage called marriage and make him like it.

No wonder he'd fought her.

No wonder he'd stopped loving her.

Dear Reader,

I know this is a hectic time of year. From the moment you cut into that Thanksgiving turkey, to the second midnight chimes on December 31, life is one nonstop *RUSH*. But don't forget to take some private time…and relax with Silhouette Desire!

We begin with *An Obsolete Man,* a marvelous *Man of the Month* from the ever-entertaining Lass Small. Next we have *The Headstrong Bride,* the latest installment in Joan Johnston's CHILDREN OF HAWK'S WAY series.

And there's *Hometown Wedding,* the first book in a fun-filled new series, JUST MARRIED, by Pamela Macaluso, a talented new-to-Desire writer. And speaking of new authors, don't miss Metsy Hingle's debut title, *Seduced.*

This month is completed with *Dark Intentions,* a sensuous, heartwarming love story by Carole Buck, and *Murdock's Family,* a powerfully dramatic offering by Paula Detmer Riggs.

Happy holidays—don't worry, you'll survive them!

Lucia Macro
Senior Editor

Please address questions and book requests to:
Silhouette Reader Service
U.S.: 3010 Walden Ave., P.O. Box 1325, Buffalo, NY 14269
Canadian: P.O. Box 609, Fort Erie, Ont. L2A 5X3

PAULA
DETMER RIGGS
MURDOCK'S FAMILY

SILHOUETTE *Desire*®
Published by Silhouette Books
America's Publisher of Contemporary Romance

SILHOUETTE BOOKS

ISBN 0-373-05898-5

MURDOCK'S FAMILY

PAULA DETMER RIGGS

discovers material for her writing in her varied life experiences. During her first five years of marriage to a naval officer, she lived in nineteen different locations on the West Coast, gaining familiarity with places as diverse as San Diego and Seattle. While working at a historical site in San Diego, she wrote, directed and narrated fashion shows and became fascinated with the early history of California.

She writes romances because "I think we all need an escape from the high-tech pressures that face us every day, and I believe in happy endings. Isn't that why we keep trying, in spite of all the roadblocks and disappointments along the way?"

For the sister of my heart, Barbara Faith Covarrubias.
I love you dearly, Barbara Jane.

One

"And now that you're out of immediate danger, Commander Murdock, I strongly recommend we schedule surgery for next week." Captain Frundt looked up from his notes expectantly.

It hurt to frown, but Cairn Murdock did it anyway. He'd learned to handle the stabbing pain in his temple whenever he changed focus, but the recurring bouts of double vision were driving him crazy. It had been that way for days now, ever since he'd opened his eyes and discovered he was in Bethesda instead of Eastern Europe where he and his outfit had been conducting a covert mission under the aegis of the United Nations.

"Bottom-line time, Doc. How long you figure I've got if I don't have the surgery?"

Dr. Frundt drew a quick breath before answering. "That's impossible to say. There are just too many variables to consider."

"Variables, meaning this chunk of shrapnel in my head just might take a notion to shift to someplace fatal?"

"Precisely. When it takes that notion can't be determined, or why. A bump on the head, even a sneeze might dislodge it. On the other hand, you could knock that hard head of yours against that wall yonder for a solid hour and get nothing more than a giant goose egg."

"Don't worry, Doc. I'm a SEAL, not a masochist."

Frundt's expression clearly registered distaste for Murdock's chosen line of work. "I'll leave that determination to the psychiatrists. My specialty is *fixing* hard heads like yours—or doing my best anyway." He cleared his throat. "In your case, we have every reason to believe surgery will enable us to remove the shrapnel successfully."

Every reason? "Yeah, right. Only, when I wake up from this successful surgery, I'll be blind. Isn't that the real bottom line?"

Frundt's gaze flickered, then held steady. Murdock almost felt sorry for the poor guy. Almost. "Yes, you'll be blind. In order to reach the sliver we will have to cut both optic nerves, which is an irreversible procedure."

Murdock wanted to ask about a third option since he wasn't crazy about the first two, but he already knew that two were all the Navy's top neurosurgeon was prepared to give him. Still, it gave him a certain satisfaction to needle the dignified captain.

"Yeah, but what about tomorrow? Say I have this operation and two months from now some genius somewhere comes up with a brand-new 'procedure' that could have saved the nerves. Then what?"

"I can't give you an answer to that, Commander."

Murdock figured he couldn't. He also figured Captain Frundt had never looked down the barrel of an enemy's AK-47, either. But he had—and survived. It had been the shell he *hadn't* seen that had exploded behind him, sending a steel souvenir into his brain.

He'd always figured to die young. Guys like him who did the country's dirty work usually did. It was part of the package he'd bought into as a gung ho ensign when he'd picked Special Ops for a career instead of a cushy billet on a warship.

He wasn't eager to die, but he wasn't afraid, either. Dicing with danger was the ultimate high; death was the penalty of losing. Ah, but the winning—that was what had kept him from being utterly bored for most of his forty-one years.

From the age of three, or maybe four, he'd been hell-bent on testing himself against the toughest challenges life could throw at him. The tops of trees were meant to be reached, no matter how dangerous the climb to get there. And the black depths of the gravel pit behind his house begged to be explored, no matter how tricky the current. As he'd grown older and stronger, the cuts and bruises his long-suffering mother clucked over constantly turned to broken bones and lacerations necessitating trip after trip to the emergency room.

He'd been twelve when he'd picked the Navy as a career—not because he liked the sea, he'd grown up in the South Carolina hills and hadn't even seen an ocean, but because he'd read an article about an elite force of mean-as-sin commandos called SEALs.

"Join the Navy and see the world," some joker had said once. And he had—places no rational man had any business being. Places with names that changed as often as their boundaries. Places with more sand than he'd believed could exist in one spot, sand that had gotten so hot at midday he'd had to wrap the grip of his rifle with wet cloth in order to keep it from searing the flesh of his hands. And places where the air was so wet a man's clothes clung like a clammy shroud and he had to sleep in a hammock slung between two trees to keep out of the mud—when he slept, that is.

Like most guys in his line of work, he'd collected his share of medals—and scars. Big ones, little ones, all the result of mistakes he'd made. Some had put him out of commission for big chunks of time, others he'd managed to patch up himself in a rain-forest village or a mountain cave.

Now that he'd already passed forty, he figured he was on borrowed time every time he climbed aboard another transport plane. On those rare occasions when he'd thought about his own death, he'd taken a certain comfort in knowing it would be quick. Not once had it dawned on him that he'd have a guy wearing a doctor's white coat and dour look passing on the sentence of death.

"Forget the surgery, Doc. I'm not into the white-cane-and-guide-dog routine."

Clear disapproval pulled Frundt's mouth down at the corners. "You're still a young man with a lot of good, productive years ahead of you."

"Doing what? Last I heard there weren't too many jobs that require my kind of experience."

"You have an impressive record. You have a lot to teach others."

Murdock figured he had about twenty minutes before the pain in his head reached the unbearable stage and he passed out again. Keeping his eyes fixed on the doctor's, he concentrated on holding his head perfectly still.

"Like I said, Captain, how long do I have? A month, a year? A couple of days? If you don't know for sure, give me your best guess."

"A few months probably, a year, perhaps. More if you're lucky. Less if you're not."

"In other words, put my affairs in order."

"That would be wise, yes."

His affairs. As in what? Telling Admiral Mac McKinley not to plan on him for any more long-term missions? Getting his XKE out of storage and ready to sell? Telling his landlady she was more than likely going to lose a tenant before the year was out?

Murdock thought of his place in Alexandria. Three rooms and a bath on the top floor of a house that had once belonged to one of Teddy Roosevelt's sons. He kept his civilian clothes there and the collection of books he read voraciously when he was in port, along with his grandfather's old twelve-gauge and a bunch of old-fashioned LPs he should have thrown out years ago.

Hell, the records weren't even his. They'd belonged to his wife, when he'd had one. He'd found them stashed in a closet after the divorce, one of the few tangible reminders of a marriage that had gone sour.

Few of his buddies even knew he'd been married. Fewer still knew he had two daughters he hadn't seen in twelve years. Sometimes he had trouble believing it himself. And then there were times, usually when he'd been on shore too long with too much time on his hands and too much booze in his belly, when he wanted to see his girls so badly it was a bloody gash on his soul. He wondered what B.J. would think if he suddenly showed up on her doorstep, demanding to see his daughters one more time before he died.

Ardeth would be fourteen now and Emily would soon be turning thirteen. If he saw them on the street, he wouldn't recognize them. Nor would they know him—not even his name.

As soon as they'd been old enough to understand, they'd been told that their mother and their real father had divorced when they'd been babies, and that he was no longer a part of their lives. When they were grown, they would be told his name and family history. Until then, Ardeth and Emily had been brought up to consider their mother's second husband, a man named Roger Dalton, as their father. It was the way B.J. had wanted it.

Maybe he shouldn't have agreed, but he had—eventually.

Regret wasn't an emotion he particularly welcomed. Come to think of it, he wasn't all that crazy about emotion, period. It clouded a man's judgment and messed up his concentration.

Action was what counted. If a man screwed up, it was up to him to take the heat—and then make sure he didn't screw up again. And if he had unfinished business, it was up to him to finish it.

"When can I get out of here?"

Frundt frowned his usual disapproval, but Murdock saw the resignation in the other man's eyes. For a four-striper, Frundt wasn't a bad guy. Just a bit too spit-and-polish for his taste, but then, what captain wasn't?

"Give us another week of your company at least, Murdock."

"I'll give you two days, and then I'm leaving. Like you said, I have things to get straight before I die."

Murdock was officially an outpatient when he entered the Pentagon three days later. The underground computer complex reminded him of a beehive, with worker bees running here and there and printers buzzing angrily. The sound made his head pound, and his muscles tense.

He found the man he'd come seeking in his usual cubby-hole, hunched over the keyboard, the frown furrows in his forehead pushing all the way to his receding hairline.

Commander Donald March had the pasty look of a man who preferred artificial light to sun. Worse, the sharp point on the end of his nose and thick black-rimmed glasses gave him an unmistakable resemblance to a mole.

His brown eyes lit up when Murdock walked in and closed the door. "Hey, Murdock, it's about time you got your behind in here to see me," he exclaimed, getting quickly to his feet, his hand already extended.

Grinning, Murdock shook the man's hand. "How's it going, Mole? Same old grind?"

"Yeah. I never should have taken those extra computer courses at the Academy."

Classmates at Annapolis, March had gotten Murdock through his math classes and Murdock had returned the favor when it had come to tactics and weapons. Tired of running up and down dormitory stairs to compare notes, they'd ended up rooming together for three years.

While others had considered him a nerd, Murdock had admired March's quick wit and lightning mind. Nobody messed with March when Murdock was around.

"I need a favor, Don, strictly off the record." He paused, knowing that what he was asking was definitely nonregulation. "I need to know all you can find out about B.J. and my kids."

March sobered, and concern replaced the laughter in his eyes. "Care to tell me why, or is it private?"

Murdock figured that death was always private. His was going to be anyway. No hovering nurses, no beeping machines or sterile white walls. Once he'd made sure his kids were happy and safe in the life their mother had chosen for them, he intended to head to the loneliest mountaintop he could find and wait for the winter snows to drift chest high—if he lasted that long. And then he intended to find the biggest drift, curl into a nice warm ball and go to sleep forever.

"Call it an attack of conscience for giving them up," he said, shifting his gaze to the bustle beyond the cubicle's windows. "Hell, Mole, maybe I'm just getting sentimental in my old age, but I need to know they're okay, that's all."

"Understood." March shifted his attention to the screen, his fingers stabbing quickly at the keys. "Does this mean you've changed your mind about not contacting them?"

"No, I gave B.J. my word."

March kept his gaze still focused on the screen in front of him. "There's a rumor going around that the doctors have beached you permanently. Any truth to that?"

"Some, yeah."

"I heard you pulled a rough one last time around. What was it, a grenade?"

"Shell fragment. Never saw it coming."

"Happens that way sometimes." March keyed a command, and the screen came alive. Sitting back, he crossed his arms and looked smug.

"There you go, Murdock. Everything ever input into a computer about that pretty lady you let get away."

"She's the one who walked out, remember?"

March clucked his tongue. "I still say you blew it, old buddy. Women like B.J. don't come along all that often, and when they do, they don't usually fall for the likes of you. If it'd been me, I would have done what I had to to keep the lady happy."

For an instant Murdock considered shoving Mole's keyboard into his big mouth, then made himself shrug the urge off. "That's ancient history, Mole. Like the man said, if you can't change it, don't sweat it."

Sympathy flashed in March's eyes, but Murdock knew his friend wouldn't put words to the thought. Knowing when to stop ragging was one of Mole's greatest talents.

Standing behind Mole's left shoulder, Murdock watched the words and numbers scroll across the screen—Social Security number, tax records, bank accounts, credit history, the life of one Barbara Jane Murdock Dalton, née Berryman. Impersonal as a legal brief and without B.J.'s vibrancy.

Now thirty-six, she'd been born and reared in Mantree, Oregon, the only child of Noah and Jane Berryman, both deceased. She was a cum laude graduate of the University of Oregon. Married to Cairn Anthony Murdock, USN, at the age of twenty-one. Divorced five years later at which time she'd been awarded sole custody of two minor daughters, ages eighteen months and seven months.

She'd remarried two years later to Mantree resident Roger Bruce Dalton. One child, a son, Richard Berryman Dalton had been born.

The boy would be four, no five now, Murdock realized. No longer a baby. He still remembered the numb shock he'd felt when her letter telling of the baby's birth had caught up with him.

The girls adore their new baby brother, Cairn. And they're such sweet sisters to him. Roger is as proud as he can be—of all three of our children. Thank you again for giving us this gift.

Pain stabbed in his head, and the words suddenly shifted and blurred, becoming two letters where before there had been one. He'd given her a lot of gifts in their time together, things, mostly. What she'd really wanted had been a normal life with a husband who worked nine-to-five at a steady job and slept at home every night. Neither of them had figured that out until it had been too late.

To her credit, she'd never complained those first few years when he'd been gone more than he'd been home. And maybe, if she hadn't insisted on having a baby, they might have made a go of it.

He'd been on a mission when B.J. had given birth to Ardeth, on another when she'd had Emily. He'd finally made it home when Emmy was a month old. By the time he'd packed his seabag for another mission, B.J. had been pregnant again.

He'd been deep in a South American jungle when she'd miscarried and nearly died. The word hadn't caught up with him for a month, and even then, he hadn't been able to make it home for another three weeks.

She still loved him, she'd said, but facing death had changed her perspective. Children needed a mother who wasn't always on edge with worry and a father who was more than an infrequent visitor in his own home. She'd given him a choice. Leave the service, or she would file for divorce.

"Why you sly fox! Now I get the picture."

Murdock opened his eyes and scowled at his friend. "What the hell are you talking about? What picture?"

March nodded toward the screen. "The ex-Mrs. Murdock is now a widow. In other words, old son, she's available."

Lightning cracked overhead as yet another spring storm swept into her part of Oregon. Safe inside the big old farmhouse, B.J. Dalton listened to the wind gusting against the windows and fervently prayed that the tender berry canes in the field would escape unscathed.

Seated across from her on the divan that had come with her family over the Oregon Trail, Garson Tremaine glanced heavenward and scowled.

Don't worry, Gar, she wanted to say. The roof might leak here and there, but it's held tight in far worse blows than this. Instead, she threw him a reassuring smile and listened patiently to the offer she'd known was coming since he'd driven up the lane an hour earlier. She owned a mountainside of trees, acres and acres of them. Douglas fir, ponderosa pine, even a magnificent stand of redwood, and Cascade Timber wanted them.

"No doubt about it, B.J.," Tremaine concluded, his hearty tone just shy of overbearing. "This is one world-class offer. All you have to do is put your signature in these two places, and Cascade will make you a very rich woman."

He placed the contract of sale and his gold pen on the coffee table well within her reach, then settled comfortably against the horsehair upholstery, his expression smug, his expectations clear. In his world money talked, and he'd just shouted at her loud and clear. Six figures for a bunch of trees that were only going to die sooner or later anyway.

That was his opinion, she reminded herself, not hers. Still, it was an opinion shared by most of her neighbors, especially those who depended upon the two Cascade mills for steady, well-paying jobs.

B.J. couldn't fault them for their concern. She liked security as well as the next person—more, perhaps, now that she was a single parent. But protecting those trees and the ecosystem they sheltered had been a passion with the Berrymans for as long as she could remember.

The trees had been there when the Indians camped by the river, and they'd been there when the weary survivors of the Oregon Trail had collapsed in the welcome shade, unable to go one more day, one more step.

When no one was around, she talked to the trees, even hugged her favorites when she felt most alone and lost. The trees were as much a part of her family as her children, and she loved them almost as much. Not even the promise of a fat bank account could tempt her to give them up.

"First let me say that I appreciate your offer, and I agree—it's very generous, but—"

"No 'buts' about it, B.J. It's more than your father made in a lifetime of farming, more than you can expect to make in yours."

Garson glanced pointedly at the frayed collar of her ragged work shirt. It had been one of Roger's, saved not for sentimental reasons, but because the extra-long sleeves protected her arms from thorns when she was in the fields.

"We're not exactly starving, Gar. And now that the kids have gotten over Roger's death, we're all pretty content with what we have."

"Didn't say you weren't, B.J., but we both know how expensive it can be to raise kids these days. Why, just getting one through college is a struggle, and you've got three to worry about."

"The girls have a trust fund for that." Thanks to Cairn Murdock's strong sense of responsibility. To her surprise and his credit, he'd done right by them, contributing even more to the fund than the amount agreed upon in the divorce settlement.

"Put it this way, B.J. You're too pretty a woman to be busting your buns in the fields day after day just to eke out a living. Not when you could be wearing silk instead of hand-me-downs."

"Silk isn't very practical for a farmer, Gar."

"Don't get me wrong, B.J. You're still a damn good-looking woman no matter what you wear." His mouth slipped into a grin so persuasive she wondered if he practiced in front of his mirror every morning when he was shaving.

"And you deserve the best, after what you've gone through these past two years, what with Roger's death and no insurance and all. Tell you true, B.J., I don't know when I've admired a woman more, which is why I talked Pop and the rest of the board into offering you such a sweet deal."

Reminding herself that she and her three kids had to live in Mantree, which was as close to a company-owned town as it could get, she managed to look thoughtful and regretful at the same time.

"Sorry, Gar, I can't accept your offer, no matter how sweet it is. Those trees are sacred."

He snorted. "Nothing is sacred when jobs are at stake. Your father might not have been smart enough to understand that, but you are."

B.J. felt a rush in her veins. Her ancestors had been Slavic, with hot tempers and strong wills that not even the brutal trials of the Oregon Trail had defeated. They might have changed their name when they became Americans, but not their temperament. Even four generations away from the old country, she had the same fire in her blood.

"Jobs, Garson?" she asked carefully. "Or Cascade's profit margin?"

"What's good for Cascade is good for the people who work for us."

Lightning flashed again, so close this time the thunder hurt her ears. A split second later rain hit the windows like hailstones.

"What about the wildlife that depends upon those trees?" she asked tersely, her eyes narrowing to focus hard on his. "What about erosion control and the beauty the trees provide? Aren't those things important, too?"

"It's hard to appreciate beauty when folks are going hungry."

B.J. felt her patience thinning. She'd been through this same argument too many times in the past year—not only with Garson and his father, Hayden, but with just about everyone she met. Friends, neighbors, even government officials were taking sides. Everyone had an opinion; no one had a solution. In the meantime, the politicians wrangled endlessly while environmentalists and timbermen squared off for a to-the-death battle in the courts.

B.J. hadn't aligned herself with any organized group. That wasn't her way and never had been. She just knew she loved the trees and intended to keep her small corner of the world intact.

"I'll tell you what," she said, smiling as she rose, "I won't try to change your mind, and you don't try to change mine, okay?"

Garson remained seated. "Okay, enough of this ecology B.S.," he said with a hint of the condescension befitting the only son and heir of the county's most powerful employer. "How much do you want?"

"My trees aren't for sale at any price. Period."

"One million, cash. In a Swiss account if that will help to ease your conscience."

"Read my lips, Gar," she said, leaning closer. "No. *N...O.*"

Garson shot forward in his chair, a mottled flush marring the perfection of his Acapulco tan. The smug smile was replaced by an impatient snarl.

"I would reconsider if I were you, little lady. Life can get pretty tough for a woman alone in these parts."

B.J. inhaled swiftly, then burst out laughing. "Oh, for heaven's sake, Gar. Stop acting like some kind of mob enforcer. You know as well as I do your father would never let you harm me. He and Dad might have squabbled over those trees, but deep down they were as close as brothers."

Tremaine took his time standing, then picked up his pen and carefully replaced it in the inside pocket of his suit coat. When he glanced up again, his features were once more composed, his expression congenial. But his brown eyes seemed to have paled to a reptilian hazel.

"Times have changed, B.J.," he said evenly. "And my father isn't running Cascade anymore. I am." He picked up his briefcase, then paused. "I want those trees, B.J., and I intend to have them—with or without your cooperation."

He left her standing alone by the old divan, telling herself that he was wrong. She would never give up those trees.

Two

Hidden by the trees along the road, Murdock rested his aching head against the seat and rolled the window of his new truck a little lower, hoping to catch a breeze. It was the second week in June, and the spring rains had finally ended.

Through the cover of leaves he watched the bright orange tractor approaching. B.J. was belted into the seat, a jaunty cowboy hat perched on her dark hair, driving the little Kubota as though it were a souped-up hot rod.

He'd been watching her place for almost a week now, since the day he'd arrived, in fact, memorizing the farm's daily routine. He knew when the workers arrived, and when they left. He knew when the school bus came in the morning and when it dropped the children off in the afternoon. By the end of his first day in Mantree, he'd had the entire perimeter of B.J.'s place for twenty miles each way firmly fixed in his head.

He'd already learned as much as Mole's data bank could tell him about the town, and in particular detail, Cascade Timber. As soon as he'd arrived, he'd headed straight for the Junction Tavern, the town's most popular—and roughest—watering hole, telling the bartender and everyone who'd listen that he'd just put in an application at the mill.

To cover his lack of actual mill experience, he'd presented himself as a logger dispossessed by the owl controversy and looking for work indoors now instead of out.

Looking the part had been a cinch. His large size and solidly muscled weight were the norm for a man accustomed to the brutal day-to-day exertion of logging. And his big hands had the requisite calluses, acquired, however, by the constant handling of a weapon instead of a chain saw.

He'd had references, forged by an expert, that had all but guaranteed a quick hire. He was to start on Monday, on the day shift at Mill Number One. Until then, he was using his time to watch and plan. From the things he'd already learned, Mantree was a powder keg just waiting for someone to strike a match.

Rumor had it that Cascade had put out the word. Anyone working for B.J. Berryman would be held in severe disfavor by the mill's management. Which meant that neither they nor any of their relatives would ever work for Cascade again.

He'd already learned what a powerful bargaining chip that could be in a place all but owned by one family. And this morning he'd noticed that only half of B.J.'s workers had shown up. He had a feeling tomorrow would see even fewer congregating outside the equipment shed to receive the day's orders from their lady boss.

At the end of the row, B.J. let the tractor idle while she swept off her hat and wiped her brow with the red bandanna she invariably wore around her neck when she was in the fields.

He'd already discovered how hard she worked, sometimes returning to the fields after dinner to finish one chore or another. As for the woman herself, he didn't want to think about the nights he'd spent wide-awake and trying not to mentally strip her out of the men's shirts she seemed to favor when she worked the fields, knotted at the waist to keep the tails from tangling in the machinery.

And her favorite jeans were shiny across the fanny from the tractor seat and sported red patches on the knees. Even through binoculars, just watching her walk from the house to the equipment shed had been an exercise in mind control.

He plowed stiff fingers through his hair. It was nearly two inches long now and thick enough to hide the scars webbing his scalp. If it weren't for the frequent headaches and occasional bouts of double vision, he might be tempted to forget the death sentence hanging over him. And then what? he reminded himself. Stay long enough to end up dead on her doorstep, or worse, a mindless babbling infant just waiting for someone to pull the plug?

Watching her now, he wondered if she ever thought of the stubborn, bad-tempered man who'd been her husband for five short years. If she did, he had a feeling it wasn't fondly.

For that reason he'd delayed contacting her. Until he was certain she and her children needed his help, he didn't intend to open old wounds. Hers or his.

But, selfish bastard that he was, he would willingly sell what was left of his soul to be allowed to make love to her one last time before he died.

B.J. slammed the door of her pickup and stalked toward the picnic grounds. Beyond the split-rail fence River Bend Park was alive with families enjoying the Fourth of July holiday at Cascade's expense.

Circling a row of pickup trucks and semi cabs, she headed for the thick shade where the partying mill workers were clustered. It hadn't rained for nearly a month, and she could smell the dust from the dozens of cars pulling in and out of the lot all morning. Already at a few minutes past noon, the gravel parking lot had soaked up enough sun to scorch the soles of her canvas high-tops.

As she neared the grassy concourse between the twin shelters, she recognized some of her former employees along with friends and neighbors, all of whom had at least one family member on the Cascade payroll.

A few waved halfheartedly when they saw her, as though they hadn't quite made up their minds to hate her. The majority of those who made eye contact, however, glared angrily before pointedly turning their backs. The snubs hurt, worse than she'd expected.

Reining her temper, she wove a path through the blankets and lawn chairs until she spied the cheery red-and-white stripes of the refreshment tent. The smell of charcoal and singed hamburger wafted toward her, along with the distinct aroma of fresh popcorn.

Her stomach churned, reminding her that she had just been sitting down to grab a quick bite of lunch when Ardeth had burst into the kitchen, sobbing. On orders from his father, Gary Tremaine had broken their date for the picnic.

B.J. had found herself in the truck and heading for the picnic grounds within minutes, her temper seething and her patience all used up.

A few paces to the left of the tent, a pickup sporting the flashy orange-and-green Cascade Timber insignia was parked near the riverbank in the deep shade of a big old birch. Ice filled the bed, cooling a huge mound of beer cans. A swarthy man with a hairy chest only partially covered by the bib of his overalls was busily handing out can after can to a steady stream of mostly male picnickers.

After a quick search, B.J. spied Garson in a group of men near the tree's trunk and veered in that direction, her head held high and her eyes straight ahead as she hurried past a clown in full regalia, a huge bouquet of helium-filled balloons bobbing wildly above his head.

As he had done for as long as she could remember, "Popo" was dispensing balloons to squealing children while their mothers snapped picture after picture. B.J. had hired that same clown for Ricky's fifth birthday just last month, and many of the children at the picnic had been among the guests. That had been B.T., she reminded herself grimly. Before Trees.

These days Ricky played alone and wondered why none of his friends came over anymore. B.J. had just about run out of excuses. Good ones, anyway.

"Hi, Mrs. Dalton," one of the boys called out in a reedy voice, and would have said more, but his mother had already bent over to shush him.

"Hi, Trent," B.J. said, slowing to bestow a special smile on the towheaded kindergartner who until recently had been Ricky's "bestest friend in the whole wide world."

"You're not welcome here, B.J.," his mother said, holding him firmly by the shoulders to keep him from greeting her with a hug the way he normally would.

Bernice Coats had been two years behind B.J. in high school. They'd served as cochairmen of the co-op preschool for the past two years, and B.J. had always considered her a friend.

B.J. stopped dead in her tracks and looked the woman in the eye. "That wasn't what you said last spring when you and Emmett had to make an emergency trip to Seattle, and you needed a place for Trent to stay while you were gone."

Bernice had the grace to look ashamed before she turned her back. Not so one of the other mothers, however. Teeth bared, she stepped forward suddenly, blocking B.J.'s path.

"Me and my Joseph have us five kids to feed, and he done got word from Mr. Tremaine Junior this week that they was gonna have to lay off a whole shift come September, all on account of you."

So that was the line Garson was putting out, B.J. thought with disgust. Talk about playing dirty.

"Mr. Tremaine has a tendency to exaggerate," she said with a calm in her voice she was far from feeling.

The woman puffed out her chest and moved closer. B.J. detected the odor of onions, stale beer and cheap cologne. "Are you selling them trees or not?"

"I've given my answer and my reasons a dozen times these past few months," she said with her most persuasive tone. "I'm sorry if you're upset, but—"

"Upset ain't the half of it!" The woman turned suddenly to include the onlookers with a sweeping gesture of one fleshy hand. "C'mon, you folks. Tell her what we think of her and her kind around here."

In the ensuing hubbub, B.J. heard herself called everything from a lousy environmentalist to an owl-lover and a traitor by people she'd known all her life. Even sweet-natured Orville Beene, who'd been her Sunday school teacher for years was now regarding her with open disapproval.

"Look, this is silly," B.J. cried. "You all know me and how much I love this community. I'm just—"

"Some kind of love, puttin' folks out of work," a rough male voice shouted above the buzz of angry voices.

B.J. sensed a change in the air around her and saw that the small group of mothers and children had swelled, forming a ragged circle around her and the woman blocking her way.

B.J. caught a movement out of the corner of her eye and turned in time to see Garson Tremaine step into the open. His expression was just short of triumphant, and B.J. realized that she'd made a tactical error in coming alone into enemy territory. Retreat, however, was out of the question. No way would she give Garson or anyone else the satisfaction of seeing her turn tail.

"Think about it," she shouted over the din. "Even if I sold my trees, *all* my trees, the timber would only keep the mill going another year at the most. In the meantime, an ecosystem that had taken centuries to perfect would be destroyed."

"So what?" a voice cried.

"Yeah, who cares about a bunch of stupid animals anyway? People are more important than any ecosystem."

B.J. turned to confront the last speaker, who, from the slurred, sloppy quality of his speech, had to be more than half-drunk. Her stomach knotted when she saw that he was Sarge Crookshank.

Known around town as an honest, hardworking man when he stayed away from the booze, the ex-Marine changed into a foulmouthed, belligerent bully when he drank, quick with his fists and not above hitting a woman. In fact, he'd served time in state prison a while back for breaking his wife's jaw.

At the moment he was looking at B.J. as though that was nothing compared to the damage he intended to do to her. A quick glance at the faces lined up against her showed that her former friends and neighbors just might let him have his way. She told herself that she was being paranoid, but at the same time, she knew her knees would wobble if she relaxed her rigid muscles.

Ignoring Crookshank's bloodshot glare took some doing, but she managed to shift her gaze to Garson Tremaine's face. His mouth twitched as their eyes met, and B.J. realized he was trying hard not to grin at her discomfort.

"I need to talk to you," she said just loud enough for him to hear.

"Why, sure, B.J.," he said with a smirk. "Go right on and talk."

"Not here, it's private."

Like most of the other men now gathered around, he was holding a can of beer. Instead of answering, he treated himself to a long guzzling swallow before lowering the can again.

"If you're here to tell me you changed your mind about selling your trees, I'm listening. Otherwise, this is a private party you're crashing."

He had the upper hand and he knew it. B.J. had two choices. Walk away now and feel like a coward. Or discuss her daughter's private pain in public.

"I won't be blackmailed," she declared.

"Who said anything about blackmail?" He turned to grin at the men ranged in a loose semicircle around him.

"Let's be real here, Garson," she said, her attention on the mill owner exclusively. "We both know you're the reason my workers quit, and now you're the one behind Gary's decision to stop seeing my daughter."

Garson shrugged, all pretense at innocence gone. His eyes narrowed, and B.J. wondered why she'd never noticed their snakelike quality before now.

"Gary's a timberman, like all the Tremaines. He knows what has to be done to maintain the quality of life folks need in these parts."

Ignoring the curious faces ringing her, she propped one fist on her hip and regarded Garson coolly. "Tell me something, Gar. How in the world does your son's breaking my daughter's heart maintain the quality of life in Mantree?"

"Maybe that's not all he should break," a male voice sang out before Tremaine could reply.

"Yeah, what's one less tree-hugger anyway?" cried another man from the back of the crowd. There was a flurry of humorless laughter, mostly masculine, followed by several crude words of agreement.

B.J. whirled, her fists clenched. Her heart was pumping fast and hard, and adrenaline sped like heat through her system, making her slightly light-headed.

"That's a despicable thing to say!" she cried.

"What's that mean?" someone called.

"Means B.J. thinks we're all a bunch of dumb hicks in these parts," answered another, a woman this time, with a snarl in her voice.

"Yeah, just 'cause most of us were too busy making a living to go off to college like she done."

Others chimed in readily, their voices strident and angry. Feeling the tension mount, B.J. searched the crowd, desperately seeking a friendly face, a sympathetic pair of eyes.

As she did, she was struck by a powerful moment of déjà vu, followed by a nagging feeling of uneasiness. For an instant, before the crowd shifted and cut off her view, she could have sworn she'd seen Cairn in the crowd, standing with his back to the trunk of a giant birch, his arms crossed over his wider-than-wide chest, his lean face in shadow.

The man was dressed in the traditional garb of a logger—wear-whitened jeans, a shirt that had once been plaid but had long since faded to the color of a rain-muted sky and worn boots. Unlike the other men, however, he was wearing a Texas-style Stetson instead of the ever-present gimme cap, and his stance was more self-assured cowboy than belligerent logger.

Because she hadn't thought about Cairn Murdock in a long time, she had to take a moment to collect her suddenly scattered thoughts. This stranger and Cairn could have been brothers, so alike had they seemed to her for an instant there.

Both had the same wide shoulders and hard, compact hips. Both had the same heavily muscled forearms and large, competent hands. But it was the quiet air of supreme self-confidence that struck her most forcefully. No one, but no one, had dared to challenge Cairn when he withdrew into himself the way this stranger seemed to be doing.

"Go home, B.J.," someone shouted. "Get on out of here."

"Get on out of the state while you're at it," another added.

She hoped a friendly smile would ease some of the tension. When it didn't, she took a step backward, only to find herself hemmed in even tighter.

It was clear now that she'd misjudged the depth of her neighbors' resentment, resentment that just needed a reason to boil over into an ugly fury. Mass hysteria was only a vague concept before. Now she was beginning to understand the power of collective emotion.

"Look, this whole thing is getting out of hand here. Those of you who know me know I'm not your enemy."

"If you ain't, who is?" Crookshank was only inches away now, cutting off her escape.

"Try certain greedy mill owners for one." She glanced toward Tremaine who was no longer grinning. "Not to mention the politicians who ignored the selling off of old growth because reelection was more important than integrity."

Crookshank glanced to his left where Garson was still standing. B.J. caught the slight nod of the mill owner's head and the sudden triumphant glint in Crookshank's eyes. Like a coyote scenting prey, his teeth bared and his eyes narrowed. If there was a human heart behind the malice she read there, it had been horribly disfigured.

"Let's you and me take a walk, Miz High-and-Mighty Dalton."

"Let's not." She took a step backward, knowing now how a deer felt during hunting season.

At the same moment a movement to her right had onlookers moving aside. In the next instant she felt a strong arm encircling her waist. As much from anger as fear, she shot an elbow in the ribs of her attacker, only to find herself jerked hard against an unyielding male body.

"Let me go, you idiot," she cried angrily, twisting enough to see the face of her assailant. It was the man she'd seen earlier.

B.J. stopped breathing.

"Cairn?" she whispered when she found breath again.

"Hello, B.J. Long time no see."

She blinked at him in growing disbelief. "What in the world are you doing here?"

"At the moment, I'm buying you some time."

He tightened his hold on her waist, the steel of his arm muscles hard against her back. His strength had always been prodigious. Now it seemed even more so.

"Got to hand it to you, Murdock," Sarge boomed drunkenly. "You got you a way with the women, but you better know right off, this one's a right handful."

Cairn grinned, and then to B.J.'s utter shock, winked at the other man broadly. "Just the way I like 'em, Sarge, if you catch my meaning."

Keeping her welded against his side, Murdock shouldered past a line of men as big or bigger. No one seemed inclined to stop him.

"Hey, where're you takin' her, buddy?" someone called. "We wanna watch the fun."

At the same time another voice shouted a crude sexual obscenity, and a roar of male laughter went up, followed by a scattering of nervous female giggles.

Sarge's rude guffaws followed them as she was ignominiously hustled past a blur of faces, her feet scarcely touching the gravel. Stumbling, she was saved from falling by the arm encircling her waist. Instead of letting go, however, he tightened his grip, keeping her prisoner. The enforced intimacy had her fuming, but his forearm was iron.

"Keep moving, honey. We're not out of this yet."

She sputtered a protest, which Murdock ignored until they reached her truck. He used his free hand to open the passenger door.

"Get in."

"I will not," she said through a tight jaw, then frowned. "How'd you know this was my truck anyway?"

"I saw you drive up. Now will you stop fighting me and get in the damned truck?"

B.J. stared at him. He'd seen her arrive, and yet he hadn't made his presence known? Did he dislike her that much? Hurt dulled some of her anger, but not all.

"I'm perfectly capable of driving myself home, thank you."

He muttered something under his breath and scooped her into his arms, depositing her on the seat so hard she bounced.

"Hey!" she cried out, only to have the heavy door slammed in her face. Murdock was around the truck and behind the wheel so fast her neck felt like a swivel, trying to keep track of him. Like most of her neighbors, she'd left the keys in the ignition. A twist of his wrist and a jerk of the gearshift, and he had the truck started and moving backward out of the parking space.

"Are you nuts?" she shouted over the roar of the engine.

He spared her a fast look before shifting to first gear. "Must be, to get mixed up with you again." His big boot hit the accelerator, and the truck shot out of the lot, stirring gravel and dust into a thick brown cloud behind them.

B.J. grabbed for the dash to brace herself against the violent jolting of the tires on the rutted lane and glared at the man behind the wheel.

"I don't know what you're doing here, and to tell you the truth, I don't much care. But this I do know—you have no right to interfere in my business."

He shifted to second. "Wrong. I have two daughters that give me that right." His tone was measured, the texture downright scary. B.J. stiffened her spine and cursed the flaw in her character that had led her, once upon a lifetime ago, to fall in love with this man.

At the crossroads, without being directed, he turned left onto the county road leading to her farm. Suspicion had her staring hard at his profile. It was still as solid and intimidating as ever. And she had a feeling, even without seeing them, that his eyes would be the color of freshly chipped flint.

He braked for a particularly dangerous curve, then accelerated so fast she banged her shoulder against the door. She grabbed the seat belt and rammed the end into the slot. Cairn had always been a fast driver, especially when he was angry. And he *was* angry.

But then, so was she.

"What's a Navy SEAL doing in a crowd of redneck loggers?" she demanded, her voice raised to a shout to be heard over the roar of the engine and the rush of the wind.

"Having a beer, which, come to think of it, I never got the chance to finish."

"That picnic was strictly for Cascade employees."

He shrugged shoulders that seemed to have grown even wider over the years. "I'm drawing a Cascade paycheck so that must make me an employee."

He glanced her way again, and she saw a definite glint of amusement in his eyes.

"Why in the world would the SEALs be interested in Cascade Timber?"

"As far as I know, they aren't."

"Then why—"

"The Navy and I have parted company."

B.J. gaped. "You're retired?"

"I've put in my papers, yeah. Bureau of Personnel just hasn't gotten around to processing them."

"But why? I mean, you always said you'd die in uniform." She'd believed him, which was one of the reasons she'd begged him to resign his commission.

His jaw tightened. "I got myself shot up the last time out, and the doctors convinced the brass to stick me behind a desk. I told 'em what they could do with that offer."

"That still doesn't explain what you're doing here."

"I had time on the books—the Navy calls it terminal leave," he said, his tone dust-dry. "You told me once I would love Oregon, so I came to see for myself."

B.J. frowned. "Let me get this straight, okay? You came to Oregon on vacation and ended up working at the mill?" She shook her head. "Surely you don't really expect me to believe a crock like that?"

"It was worth a shot." His grin came hesitantly, as though it had lain dormant for a lot of years.

B.J. suddenly felt herself rocked by a wash of nostalgia so powerful she stopped breathing. She'd fallen in love with that naughty Huck Finn grin before she'd even met the man behind it. Like sunshine flashing between storm clouds, it had teased and startled at the same time. When things had started to go wrong, the grin she'd loved had taken on a cynical slant that had made her want to scream. Or cry her eyes out.

"Cairn, I'm serious," she said with added severity. "Why are you here?"

He returned his gaze to the road, but not before she saw the amusement disappear. "You mean, why did I break my promise never to show my face in the same county with my girls, don't you?"

B.J. wondered if she was imagining the bitter twist to his words. "If that's the way you want to put it, yes."

He slanted her a long, cool look, his expression suddenly unreadable. B.J. forced her gaze to hold steady on his. In the past, she'd lost every contest of will between them. This time she was determined to hold her own.

His mouth quirked. "You're right. I owe you an explanation and now's as good a time as any." He checked the mirrors, then swerved the truck to the shoulder and killed the engine.

The road was quiet, and the only sound in the cab came from the chirping of tree toads in the distance. Even the wind seemed to have died.

B.J. realized that she was as nervous as she'd been the first time she and Cairn had been alone like this. She'd been a brand-new college graduate with a year's appointment as a legislative aide to Oregon's senior senator. Cairn had been one of several junior naval officers attending the senator's party in honor of a retiring admiral.

He'd driven her home. On the way they'd stopped by the Potomac to watch the city lights. A spring squall had come up suddenly, beating down on the Jaguar's ragtop in a steady hypnotic rhythm.

She could still remember the sparkle of the lights on the water and the scent of cherry blossoms in the air as he'd pulled her ever so gently into his arms.

Lightning had flashed then, illuminating the demand in his dark eyes, and she could still feel the shivery excitement that had run over her.

Watching him now, she realized just how naive she'd been to think she could actually take a wild hawk, confine him to a cage called marriage and make him like it.

No wonder he'd fought her.

No wonder he'd stopped loving her.

Leaving him hadn't been as easy for her. It had taken months before she stopped waking up with scratchy eyes and a lump in her throat. More months after that to get over the guilt of a failed marriage and the ache of a broken heart.

"I'm waiting," she reminded him when the silence grew uneasy.

Murdock made himself look at her. Her face was in shadow, making the slant of her cheekbones even more pronounced. She'd told him once that she had Indian blood, and even though her hair was a soft golden brown instead of black, it was as thick and straight as an Indian maiden's. He remembered how she'd tried and tried to curl the ends under, only to give up and confine the long thickness into a sleek braid that swished enticingly whenever she walked.

Her hair was shorter now, shining with health and streaked lighter by the sun where it brushed the curve of her jaw. He knew it would feel like sun-warmed glass against his palm.

"You want the truth, here it is. You're in trouble, and you don't seem to know just how much."

"I know there's some animosity, but it'll pass. In the meantime—"

"In the meantime, you and my daughters just might end up by the side of the road bleeding your guts out."

B.J.'s jaw dropped. "Now I know why you left the Navy, Murdock. They kicked you out for being certifiably insane."

He gave her an assessing look that went on far too long before he dropped his gaze to the seat between them. The sudden silence went from uneasy to tense before he removed his hat and placed it on the seat between them. Without it, he seemed more like the sexy, irresistible man she remembered, and she wanted to tell him to put it back on.

"I'm not insane, B.J. Just a guy who's spent half his life putting out brushfires started by hotheads like Tremaine and his goons."

"Oh, come on now, Cairn. You make it sound like Gar is Hitler or Saddam Hussein, for heaven's sake. And as for goons, I admit that Sarge Crookshank and a lot of other men in the Northwest look, well, goonlike, but believe me, they're not. I grew up with a lot of those men, and most of them are really sweet souls."

"Those 'sweet souls' intend to do whatever it takes to get your trees."

B.J. stared at him. If the nail-hard look in his eyes was anywhere close to accurate, Cairn believed the things he was telling her. That didn't mean he was right. In fact, she was sure he wasn't. On the other hand, she had always been too trusting in her life.

"How do you know that?"

He shrugged off her skepticism in the same way he'd once shrugged off her fears for his safety. "I asked a few questions and listened to the answers. Sarge isn't what you'd call subtle about his intentions."

"Neither is Gar or a lot of other people, but that doesn't mean there's a big bad conspiracy against me."

"No? Then how's this strike you? Two years ago Garson Tremaine started bidding for your trees. Your husband was the one who turned him down that time, and now he's dead."

She stared, not really sure how to respond. If she wasn't certain Cairn was as rational and cool under fire as anyone she'd ever met, she would swear he was indeed crazy.

"Roger was killed when he surprised a couple of transients breaking into his pickup. He'd been cutting up a fallen oak for firewood and from the evidence had been coming back to the truck for more oil for his chain saw. The marshal said those boys were probably hitchhiking and saw the truck parked alongside the road."

"Transients who just happened to be carrying a sawed-off shotgun. Doesn't that strike you as just a tad improbable?"

She flinched visibly. "Thanks for reminding me," she said in a hollow voice. "I'd almost forgotten."

Her face had paled, making the freckles stand out like gold raindrops, and her lips had taken on a sad line. Way to go, slick, he told himself in disgust. He hated feeling helpless almost as much as he hated screwing up. Around B.J. he was always doing both.

"Look, B.J., the bottom line is this. You need someone to work your fields and watch your back, and since I don't see a line forming anytime in the near future, I'm your best bet."

"In the first place, you don't know anything about berry farming—"

"I didn't know anything about mill work when I started, and I've already gotten a raise."

"—and in the second place, I'm sure I can find more workers. I'll go to the job bank again, maybe sweeten the incentives. A bonus for each day's work, another dollar per hour—something."

"Fine. Do that. I can use the help."

Her eyes heated. "How many times do I have to tell you? I don't need your help."

"Are you willing to bet your children's safety on that?"

B.J. inhaled swiftly. That he could even think such a thing of her stung. "I would never do that," she exclaimed softly. *"Never."*

Still, she remembered the manic glint in Sarge Crookshank's eyes and shuddered. Even now she could remember the icy slide of fear down her back when she realized just how vicious he could be. And if he went after her girls... Pride was one thing. Foolish pride was another.

"Congratulations," she muttered, looking drained all of a sudden. "You've made your point very well."

He wanted to hold her and tell her he was coming on so strong because he didn't have time for subtlety and finesse, but even if he reached for her, it wouldn't help either of them.

"Does that mean I'm hired?"

She nodded, too discouraged to argue. Murdock might be an alarmist and even a touch paranoid, but if there was any chance at all her children would be at risk, she would play hostess to the devil himself to keep them safe.

"I pay eight dollars an hour. Work starts at seven sharp, rain or shine."

"Agreed. And you can put the money into the girls' college fund."

B.J. slumped back against the seat, only to find Cairn watching her with eyes narrowed against the afternoon sun. The wind had picked up again, ruffling his hair into a little-boy tumble that somehow seemed incongruous with a face that could only belong to a man who'd left boyhood behind a long time ago.

It struck her that he'd given up a lot to serve his country. More, she understood with sudden insight, than perhaps he even realized. The idealistic young man she'd loved had matured into a hard-bitten, cynical fighting machine.

"Since you seem to have everything arranged your way so far, there's something I need to get straight," she said firmly.

"What's that?"

"I don't want the girls any more upset than they already are."

"Meaning what exactly?"

Meaning I don't want them falling in love with you and then watching you walk away again. "Meaning I don't expect you to tell them that it's your name on their birth certificates."

"I agreed to stay out of the girls' lives so that they could grow up with one father—Roger Dalton. Now that he's no longer in the picture, that promise is nullified."

She went totally still. "Are you saying...surely you don't intend to just barge into the girls' lives and play daddy after all these years?"

His eyes took on a disinterested look, a sure sign he was anything but. "Would that be so wrong?"

She had a sudden picture of him holding Ardeth for the first time. She'd never seen a man so enraptured.

"Ask me tomorrow when I've had a chance to think. Right now I keep thinking the girls have been upset enough in the last couple of years. We all have."

He reached for the key and fired the engine to life. "I agree," he said before putting the truck into gear. "I'm not here to make problems. Not for you or the girls, or for me. As far as they're concerned, I'm just a guy who works for you."

Three

B.J.'s house was typical of Oregon farmhouses—big and white and ugly. Whatever style the original builder had intended had been altered by haphazard additions over the years. Only the deep sheltering porch and the intricate gingerbread on the gables attested to its age, and even those had probably been added long after the place had been built.

Like a beloved family heirloom, the place was well kept, with the flower beds bordering the house full of color and carefully weeded and the grass newly mowed. A lovingly tended row of rosebushes separated the lawn from the fields beyond.

When was the last time he'd actually smelled roses? Murdock wondered. Or noticed them growing? It struck him that he couldn't remember. But ask him to identify different kinds of explosives by their smell in the darkest of rooms and he get ten out of ten. At the moment, that and a buck fifty would get him a beer at the Junction.

"Uh-oh," B.J. said in a worried tone. "Looks like we have a welcoming committee of one."

Murdock had already spied the girl perched on the top step. As soon as the truck rounded the lane's last curve and came into sight of the house, she shot to her feet and bounded down the steps toward them.

It was Emily, the daughter with her mother's dark hair and eyes. Ardeth was blond, like him, with his gray eyes and stubborn mouth.

Emily had been seven months old and sound asleep when he'd said goodbye to her. Remembering, he felt a tightness gathering in his chest and a rough tickle in this throat.

Along with her coloring, she had her mother's slight build and an athletic, energetic stride. He'd pegged her as a tomboy the moment he'd laid eyes on her again and had wondered then if Roger Dalton had taught her to throw a curve or scale a tree to the very top without taking a tumble.

"That's Emily."

He nodded. Letting her know he'd been watching the house and its inhabitants for weeks now didn't seem all that wise at the moment. "Looks like she's got something on her mind to me."

"Em's always got something on her mind," B.J. murmured, watching Cairn's jaw go tight and his mouth tense. He had stayed away, but he still cared. "She's turned into a true nester, like me. Ardeth is more of a rebel."

"Like me." His tone mocked her—and himself.

"Yes, like you," she said softly. "In many ways, but not all."

He pulled the truck to a stop in the shade of a massive pin oak by the equipment shed and killed the engine. Outwardly calm, he felt his heart in his throat, beating machine-gun fast.

"What took you so long?" Emily called to her mother as she skidded to a halt. Vitality seemed to crackle from her like electricity. Dressed in skintight shorts and a floppy shirt, she was already showing signs of her mother's charm. Some poor boy would fall hard for her someday soon, if he hadn't already. "I've been waiting for *hours.*"

B.J. remained unruffled by her daughter's pique. "I got hung up. And for the record, sweetheart, I haven't been gone for 'hours.' "

"Well, it seemed like it, what with Ardie in her room bawling her eyes out, and Ricky bugging me every five minutes to take him swimming."

"Why didn't you?"

Emily flipped her hair back, and Murdock saw B.J., twenty-one and so lovely he'd felt poleaxed. "Because *you* said to stay in the house till you got back, that's why."

Her gaze shifted toward the man seated so still and alert next to her mother. "Hi."

"Hi yourself." He made a stab at the kind of casual grin he'd never quite mastered and had a feeling it still needed more work.

"I'm Emily. Who're you?"

Direct and to the point. He liked that in the kid. What he didn't like were the lies he was going to have to tell her. Before he could frame the first one, however, B.J. leaned forward to intercede. "This is Cairn Murdock, sweetie. He's going to be working for us for a while."

"Oh yeah?" Black eyes narrowed now, Emily studied his face thoroughly, then, seemingly satisfied, nodded. "In that case, Mom probably warned you about us. I mean, about how bossy Ardie can be and how Ricky will pester the daylights out of you if you let him. Me, I'm completely perfect, but I'm also the middle kid, which means you have to pay more attention to me." She grinned triumphantly, breaking off a piece of his heart.

"How do you figure that?"

"Easy. See, Ardie is the oldest and so she gets more privileges—"

"And more responsibilities," B.J. interjected wryly.

Emily tossed her bangs out of her eyes, obviously undaunted. "—and Ricky is the baby, so naturally he's spoiled rotten, you know?"

"I hear that happens sometimes, yeah."

Needing to move, he opened the door and stepped down. Moving back a step, Emily immediately focused her sights upward. He figured she was just shy of five feet and no more than eighty-five pounds soaking wet. A pint-size package of dynamite for anyone to handle, especially a man more used to hanging around with guys the size of linebackers.

"How about you, Mr. Murdock? Do you have kids?"

"A couple. They live with their mother, and it's Cairn." No more rank, no more responsibilities. No one to care where he went or why.

"Sounds like you're divorced."

He nodded curtly, thinking that his old man would have loved this kid. She had the makings of a born prosecutor, just like Sean Murdock, Esquire.

"How long?"

"Pardon?"

"How long since your divorce?"

"Ten, twelve years."

He circled the truck, intending to open the door for B.J., only to have Emily follow on his heels like a persistent puppy. "That's pretty long to be single. I mean, you're kinda old, I know, but you're still a good-looking guy. Sorta Clint Eastwood, only bigger and blonder, you know? I bet you have lots of girlfriends." She slid a quick glance toward her mother who scowled.

"That's enough, Em," B.J. ordered sternly, stepping down and slamming the door behind her. "You're embarrassing Cairn."

Emily cocked her head in a perfect imitation of her mother. His heart did a slow tumble. "Ah, Mom, I'm just being honest."

"Which is certainly admirable, darling," B.J. intoned soberly before giving her second child a hug. "And I wouldn't want you to change for the world, only sometimes I wish you had inherited more of your mother's tact."

"Yeah, right!" Emily hooted, clearly unimpressed.

"Watch it, you, or you'll be cleaning the bathrooms for a month," B.J. teased, taking a swat at her daughter who bounded sideways, laughing.

"Okay, okay, I give!"

Standing to one side watching, Murdock felt like the outsider he was and always would be. The path not taken, he thought. What a crock to think it wouldn't come back to rip into his gut like hot lead.

"Where's your luggage?" Emily asked, nodding toward the pickup's empty bed. He was grateful for the question. It helped focus his mind on his mission.

"At my place."

"Where's that?" He should have known she wouldn't give up without all the answers.

"In town. I'm bunking temporarily in a place I rent by the week."

"Cairn hadn't planned to move in today," B.J. hastened to intercede again. "Besides, Jack hasn't moved out of the foreman's cottage yet, and—"

"Oh yes, he has," Emily exclaimed with a disgusted look. "You weren't even to the end of the lane before he started piling his tools and junk in his truck. Me and Ardie tried to stop him, but he wouldn't listen. Just kept taking things out of drawers and throwing them into trash bags." She made a face. "The place is a mess, and it smells bad, too. Like a whole pile of Ricky's dirty socks."

She started to say something else, but was distracted by something she must have heard. "Hear that? Is that the phone?" she asked, cocking her head.

B.J. heard the distant ring then, and from the sudden excitement in her eyes, so did Emily. "Maybe that's Pauline," she cried before sprinting for the house.

B.J. watched her go in silence. Glancing up, she caught Cairn looking down at her. His hands were in his pockets now, and his stance was arrogant male. All he needed was the starched white uniform to complete the picture she'd carried of him for years.

Lord, but he'd been handsome, a charming rogue with mischief in his eyes and seduction on his mind. He'd had a gift of gab so outrageous it had been irresistible, and a fluid, lean-hipped walk that had had her regretting her virginity.

What woman wouldn't have fallen for a man like that? Especially when she caught a glimpse of the sweet, giving teddy bear behind the sex appeal.

It was only later that she saw the other side of that sweet generosity—a cold, ruthless dedication to duty that turned the man she loved into a killing machine. She'd sworn then that her children would never know that man existed. It was a decision she'd never regretted. Nor could she allow herself to regret it now.

"Who's Pauline?" he asked when Emily disappeared behind a banging screen door.

"Pauline Kurtz, Em's best friend. Or she was, before all this started. Now, all of a sudden, Pauline doesn't want to have anything to do with Em. Won't even sit next to her on the school bus." She sighed. "I guess I can't blame her too much, though. Her father is swing shift foreman for Cascade."

Murdock recalled the man from the Junction—quiet guy, drank beer with a rye chaser. He ran a good six-two, and weighed in at one-ninety, not the sort to make war against women and little girls. Still, Murdock had been fooled before.

"Sounds like the man could use a lesson in ethics." He thought he'd spoken quietly and was surprised by the alarm that leapt into her eyes.

"Don't you dare!" she ordered with a real bite to her voice, and he wondered what she would do if he covered that tart little mouth with his. He contented himself with a shrug.

"You're the boss."

"Exactly." Her lips curved, raising all sorts of other questions he didn't want to answer. "Besides," she said self-consciously, "Gar would only have you arrested, and I don't have money to spare for bail."

"Problems?"

"A seasonal shortage. We'll be fine as soon as the crop gets to the canneries."

She shifted her feet and glanced again toward the house, as though reluctant to face the more difficult problems waiting behind the sparkling facade. He wasn't sure he blamed her.

Doing the impossible was his specialty. Only thing was, he was usually wearing full field gear and armed to the teeth when he went at it. Without them, he felt naked. Vulnerable. It wasn't a feeling he liked, nor one that he would ever admit to.

"I could just smack Garson Tremaine for what he's done to my babies," she muttered as though to herself.

Murdock had darker thoughts about the man. "Standing up for something isn't always easy."

"True, but when you're a kid, it's hard to understand that. It's especially hard for Ardie. She and Garson's son, Gary, were going steady—or what passes for that these days—until he broke it off on orders from his father. That's one of the reasons I went to see Gar today."

"I heard."

He watched a calico cat preening herself in the sunshine. From the looks of her swollen belly, she was just about ready to have kittens. Life goes on, he thought, no matter what mistakes guys like him made.

"I shouldn't have gone. It was a dumb idea, but Ardie came home crying and I reacted like a typical overprotective mother."

"Overprotective, maybe. Typical, never."

Her eyebrows bunched over eyes suddenly filled with suspicion. "Is that good or bad?"

He met her eyes long enough to feel the pull in his belly before looking away. "Definitely good."

Pleased and yet clearly unsettled, she drew a long breath. "It'll be all over town tomorrow, especially the part where you came out of the crowd to haul me away like a sack of potatoes."

"Maybe I should have thrown you over my shoulder. Might have made a better story."

"Don't worry, it'll be good enough as it is." She threw back her shoulders and straightened her spine. He could almost see her pull the armor over herself again, ready to take on all comers.

Shading her eyes with one hand, she directed his attention to a wooded corner of the main yard. Nestled under the trees was a small building about the size of a two-car garage, with rough weathered planks for sides and corrugated tin for a roof. Someone had planted roses on either side of the only door, providing a vivid splash of red against the silvered wood.

"That's the foreman's house there. It's only two rooms and a bath, but it's not a bad place, once we get it cleaned up. In fact, it was the original cabin, built by my great-great-

great-grandfather. Granddaddy added plumbing in the twenties, and Dad put in electricity in the fifties. Roger and I fixed up it as a sort of retreat when we got married. Our honeymoon cottage, he liked to call it.''

Her eyes grew soft, and a faint smile played around her mouth. It didn't take much imagination to figure out why. Only years of rigorous self-discipline kept him from telling her exactly how little interest he had in her life with the man who'd replaced him.

"Sounds like a palace compared to some of the places I've called home. The last one came with bedbugs and a path to the river that was usually occupied by a poisonous snake or two."

The soft light faded from her eyes. Bastard that he was, he was glad to see it go.

"It will need to be cleaned. And there's not much furniture. A table and a couple of chairs, an old couch that probably should be replaced, and of course, a bed." Like their first apartment, she realized suddenly, and came to a sudden stop.

She had loved every shabby square inch of that old walk-up because she and Cairn had lived there together. Day after day, she'd scrounged around secondhand stores in the city for furniture to refinish and fabric to make drapes. And at night, when the dinner dishes were draining and the lights were low, they'd drunk jug wine and made love on the ugly-duckling couch she'd turned into a gorgeous gingham swan.

"Well, anyway, the cabin goes with the job," she repeated, her voice cool and matter-of-fact, the way it always was when she was working at hiding her feelings. "If you'd prefer living in town, that's fine, too."

"I'll take the cabin. That trailer I've been living in reminds me of a submarine. Makes me feel like a sardine."

She turned her head to glance once more at the cabin. He'd already noticed the tiny emerald studs gleaming in her ears, and now as they flashed a brilliant green in the sunlight, he wondered if Roger had given her those earrings.

When he felt his jaw tighten, he forced his mind back to the mission. First things first, and that meant making sure he won her over to his way of thinking as quickly as possible.

"How many employees do you usually have?" he asked when her gaze came his way again.

"Three permanent, as many as fifteen during picking season. Why?"

He shrugged. "I just wondered how busy I'm going to be."

B.J. found herself smiling. Somehow the idea of Murdock swapping his combat fatigues for overalls and his assault rifle for pruning shears didn't quite mesh. "Let me put it this way, Cairn. You're not going to have a lot of time to get bored."

He smiled a little at that. "You make it sound like you don't think I can keep up."

She knew better. "I think you can probably do the work of three if you set your mind to it. The question is, why bother, if you're just here to provide security until this is settled?"

"I'm out of the Navy, remember? I need the work."

"I doubt that, but I'm too tired to argue." She paused, looking past him toward the dark wash of trees in the distance. "Who would have thought I'd end up a militant?" Her lips curved. "I've always hated violence."

"Most people do. That's why governments invented guys like me to do the dirty work for them."

He watched her eyes cloud, then grow reluctantly curious. "Is that how you saw your job? As dirty work?"

He moved one shoulder. He'd taken a bullet there once, in Beirut. "Wars, even the undeclared ones, are always messy. Dying isn't pretty."

He could say more—about the hot smell of blood spurting from burst arteries or the gristly whiteness of splintered bone poking through torn flesh and how a man, just to keep sane, had to shut off the part of himself that felt anything deeply, even love. But that would be breaking the cardinal rule of the soldier—never explain, never complain.

"No, death isn't pretty." Her mouth jerked. "I never understood that before, not until I saw Roger lying there by the side of the road." Her shoulders slumped momentarily, then straightened. "Do you really think Gar Tremaine had something to do with his death?" Just thinking he might made her skin crawl.

"Let's say it would be foolhardy not to."

"Perhaps you're right, even though I hate the very idea that someone I grew up with could be so callous." She drew a long breath. "Gar's father and mine were close friends. I wonder what he would say if I went to him for help."

"Give it a try if you have to. Me, I believe in the apple theory, the part about not falling far from the tree."

"You're probably right. I can't imagine Gar would dare do anything his father hadn't already approved." She inhaled slowly and just a bit defiantly.

"I hate this. I mean, I *really* hate it." Proud of the calm in her tone, she readjusted her focus and found herself locked into his calm, assessing gaze. Those slate-colored eyes had seen a world of violence and suffering and yet, they seemed to reflect the straightforward acceptance of a man who tried to make a difference.

Murdock wasn't an easy man to hate, even if he had once all but ripped her apart inside. Nor, she was discovering, was he an easy man to forget. Not when just being close to him had a slow, lazy sensation curling up her spine.

"Cairn, about the girls?"

"What now?" His tone was dangerous, his eyes suddenly hard cold stone.

"I have no objections to your spending time with them while you're here," she said without quite meeting those eyes. It was easier to maintain control that way. "Without telling them who you are, of course."

"Aren't you afraid I'll slip up, maybe let them know we knew each other in another life?"

Remembering just how well he'd known her and she'd known him had her drawing in a hasty breath. "I'd be lying if I said I wasn't apprehensive. But you *are* their father, and there have been times when I've had second thoughts about asking you to stay away." Admitting that was difficult, even to herself.

He cocked his head, looking thoughtful, and then his firm mouth softened just enough to give his face a rough charm.

"Like you told me once, I was the world's worst husband and father." The self-deprecating drawl had her lips curving before she realized it.

"Maybe not the worst," she murmured. "But close." She laughed softly, but her eyes were sad. "It seems so long ago, our marriage. Sometimes I would think I dreamed it all—until one of the girls would laugh like you or get that stubborn look between her eyebrows, and then I'd remember."

To her utter dismay, her eyes filled with unexpected—and unwanted—tears, and her mouth wobbled when she tried to smile. "Oh Cairn, I wish... maybe if we'd tried harder."

Because he couldn't stop himself, he knuckled a stream of tears from her cheek. She still had freckles on her nose. And the longest eyelashes he'd ever seen. They had always felt like tiny feather dusters against his cheek when she kissed him.

"No second thoughts, sweetheart. What's done is done." He flattened his palm and thought she leaned against it just a little. "Besides, you did try. I didn't."

"I think that's what hurt the most. The fact that you wouldn't bend for me, not even a little."

"I wanted to. I figured out later it just isn't in me to compromise about anything. Maybe that's why I ended up in the military, where things are pretty much black and white, without a lot of room for argument."

"Now that you're a civilian maybe that will change."

"I'm too old to change."

"You're not old. Just seasoned."

He smiled a little. "You haven't changed at all. You're still the prettiest girl at the party. And the sexiest."

Her cheeks turned pink.

"Cairn..."

"Don't worry, honey. I'm not going to make a pass at you."

"I... didn't think you were."

"Yes, you did. Maybe I did, too."

It would be so easy to kiss her now while she was feeling sentimental and just a bit sad. And then what? he thought. Even if he could talk her into giving him another chance, he'd only end up leaving again, this time in a box.

B.J. saw the change in his face a split second before he withdrew his hand and stepped backward. The walls were up again, and the longing in his eyes had hardened away.

"If you have no objection, I'd like to borrow the truck for an hour or so. I need to collect my things and notify personnel that I'm no longer on Cascade's payroll."

"No, no objection," she murmured, turning away. It wasn't easy to keep her back straight and her head high after making such a sentimental fool of herself, but she managed.

The Junction was jammed with picnic-goers determined to keep the beer buzz going long after the party was over. The noise battered his ears and jarred his head, and the thick smoke had his gut churning.

He thought of roses and freshly mowed grass, and a woman who hated violence. A sudden fierce longing to be smelling those roses with her at his side took him by surprise. Banishing it took some doing, but he managed.

Crossing to the bar, he felt the stares and curious looks directed his way. One or two of his fellow workers called ribald greetings. Knowing what they had to be thinking had his jaw set and his blood icing.

Sarge was at the bar, in his usual place. Instead of his usual beer, however, Whitey Whitlock, the bar's owner, had just served him a double whiskey neat. Murdock was pleased to see that the man didn't look drunk. He wanted Sarge aware and alert when he did what he'd come to do.

As soon as he spied Murdock, his eyes lit up, and his ugly face split into a lascivious grin. "Hey, Murdock!" he boomed loud enough to carry all the way to the street. "Didn't 'spect to see you back so soon. C'mon over here and tell me what that tight-assed bitch was like between the sheets."

Murdock knew a dozen different ways to kill, most of them quiet and swift, some so skilled not a hair on his target's head would be ruffled. But Sarge deserved a different kind of death, the kind that had a man praying for a bullet long before the end.

He let his mind toy with the details long enough to vent the worst of his rage. The rest he put into his fist when it connected with Sarge's jaw.

Sarge's head snapped back as if it were fastened to his neck by a spring, and his face took on a stupefied look right before his eyes rolled back in his head and he toppled from the stool like a felled tree.

"Damn it," someone muttered, followed by a spate of foul epithets.

"What the hell did you do that for?" Whitey demanded.

Murdock swept the room with a cold deliberate stare that slowly won him the silence he wanted. Blood spurted from a split knuckle on the hand that still formed a fist, and a flare of hot pain all but convinced him he'd broken something. He would deal with that later. Right now he had a message to send.

"Anyone who tries to get to B.J. Dalton or her family will have to go through me. Tell Sarge that when he wakes up, and while you're at it, give the same message to Garson Tremaine next time he feels like humiliating someone in public."

Using his left hand, he picked up the untasted whiskey, poured half over his still bleeding hand and downed the rest. No one said a word as he walked through the crowded bar and out the door.

B.J. circled the bed, smoothing wrinkles from the old woolen blanket she'd just spread over the clean sheets. The odor of camphor rose from the heavy material to tickle her nostrils, and she sneezed. Disinfectant and mothballs, she thought, sneezing again. She hated smelling either one.

"I hope that smell doesn't drive Cairn away before he even starts," Emily muttered as she bent to sweep the last of the dirt into the dustpan. The phone call had turned out to be a wrong number, and Emily's mood had grown steadily worse ever since.

"Don't start," B.J. warned. Her back hurt, and she had a feeling her tolerance for humor had sunk to an all-time low. Finding that Emily had measurably underestimated the filth in the cabin had been bad enough. Knowing that Cairn would soon be sleeping in the same bed where she'd slept with Roger was worse. Worst of all was not understanding why she couldn't get out of her mind the thought of him lying naked and virile between these same sheets.

Grabbing a dust rag, she wiped down the cast-iron headboard with vigorous strokes. At the same time she kept a watch through the window for the truck.

She'd gotten over him by sheer grit and determination. It had taken time and an enormous amount of energy, but she'd finally succeeded.

Discovering that he was still sexy enough to make her toes curl was unsettling, but nothing she couldn't handle. Besides, he was here because of his daughters, not her. She was just their mother, and no matter what, she wasn't about to let herself read anything else into those fleeting glimpses she'd gotten of a gentler, kinder man beneath the hardened warrior's shell.

"Mommy, I wanna go swimming!" Ricky was perched on one of the kitchen chairs, kicking one of the table legs with the toes of his sneakers. A boom box sat nearby, tuned to a hard-rock station the girls loved and B.J. detested but tolerated for their sakes.

"I've already told you three times, Richard," she said, shaking out the dust rag. "Em's going to take you—just as soon as she finishes sweeping the floor and taking out the trash. And stop kicking that table. It's rickety enough as it is."

Ricky scowled, but he stilled his feet. "It's hot in here."

"Have a glass of water. There are clean glasses in the cupboard."

"I want cream soda."

"You can have juice. You know where we keep it." B.J. arched her back, trying to work out some of the soreness, wincing when she failed.

Still pouting, Ricky climbed from the chair and left the room, heading for the main house, dragging his feet as he went.

"Make sure you get the fridge door closed all the way," she shouted after him, then stifled a sigh. She knew she had neglected him this summer, but she tried to lessen the guilt by reminding herself that she had no choice. Still, because he was the youngest, he understood least.

"Bathroom's clean," Ardeth said as she came into the bedroom carrying a bucket and a mop. She'd dried her tears and applied fresh makeup, but the puffiness around her eyes gave her a wounded look that tore at B.J.'s conscience. "And I'm telling you right now, Mom, I expect extra pay for scraping the tobacco gunk off the window."

B.J. shot her a warning look, which her daughter pointedly ignored. "I hope this new guy doesn't smoke."

"He doesn't," B.J. answered without thinking. A man whose body was a weapon didn't take chances on harming it.

Ardeth propped the mop against the wall and shifted the pail to the other hand. "How do you know he doesn't? Did you ask about that as part of the hiring interview?"

"Something like that." B.J. gave the pillow one last plump, then turned away. She cast another quick look through the window, hoping to see her truck coming up the lane, but the lane remained stubbornly empty.

"How do you know this guy isn't an ax murderer or an escaped criminal?" Ardeth shouted from the kitchen where she'd gone for more ammonia to add to the water-filled pail.

"Woman's intuition," B.J. shouted back. An ax murderer she could handle. Cairn was a worse sort of problem—a man who had suddenly reminded her that she hadn't buried her sex drive when she'd buried Roger.

"Besides he doesn't look like an ax murderer," Emily informed her sister in a knowing tone.

"Oh yeah? How do you know what an ax murderer looks like, ditz?"

"Because I watch the same TV shows you watch, dodo-head."

"I don't know when, since you spend so much time looking in the mirror for zits." Ardeth reappeared with the ammonia bottle in hand and a smirk on her face.

"At least, when I look, I don't find any—not like someone I know."

"That's a lie!"

B.J. drew a fast breath before wading in. "Stop it, you two. One battle at a time, okay? And right now we need to pull together, or we just might find ourselves covered in chicken feathers and riding out of town on rails."

Emily and Ardeth exchanged looks before Ardeth dumped ammonia into the water, adding to the mix of strong smells. "Isn't that a little extreme?" Ardeth said with the exaggerated parental tolerance B.J. had come to expect from her eldest.

"Don't ask me. I'm just the mother here. And turn down that music!"

Emily lowered the volume on the boom box a smidgen, then aimed the business end of the broom at a thicket of cobwebs overhead.

"It's okay, Mom," she said, wiping them from her face where they'd fallen. "Ardie is just upset about Gary, that's why she's being such a pill."

"Don't mention that jerk's name ever again," Ardeth ordered, squeezing water from the mop. "As far as I'm concerned, he's history. Period."

Mop in hand, she stalked to the cabin's only closet and jerked open the door, only to leap back shrieking. The mop flew from her hand. "Watch out, there it goes!"

The small brown field mouse streaked between Ardeth and her mother, heading straight for the door Ricky had left open when he'd departed.

Emily giggled. "Let's hope the new hired man likes company."

Poised for flight, Ardeth peered into the closet's musty interior, paying particular attention to the dusty space at the bottom, which still bore the marks of the previous tenant's clutter. "Maybe we should turn Patches loose in here for a few hours, just in case he doesn't."

Emily handed her sister the mop. "Better not. That closet's the perfect size for a cat delivery room."

Ardeth made a face. "What's this new guy look like anyway?" she asked, swabbing the wide wooden planks.

"Like a combination of Dirty Harry and the guy who used to advertise cigarettes on all the billboards, only bigger. Isn't that right, Mom?"

"If you say so."

For the past six months or so, her girls had been urging her to date again. She'd resisted, not because she was still mourning Roger, but because she hadn't met anyone tempting enough to disrupt her already busy routine. And she still hadn't, she reminded herself as she bent to dust the rungs of one of the chairs.

Ardeth plunged her mop into the bucket, then wrung it dry again. "Mom doesn't like macho types, remember?"

"She must have liked this one or she wouldn't have brought him home." Emily interrupted her assault on another nest of webs to look over her shoulder at her mother. "I saw you sneaking looks at him when he wasn't looking, Mom." She grinned. "And he said he wasn't married, remember?"

"Not really." B.J. finished one chair and started on the other.

"I bet he's good in bed."

B.J. straightened too quickly and banged her head on the table. It was the last straw.

"Ardeth, Emily, pay attention, please! I am not, repeat, not interested in an affair with Cairn Murdock or anyone else. And I would appreciate your not throwing out hints about the appalling lack of romance in your mother's life."

The girls looked at each other, then grinned. "But, Mom, we're just thinking about your declining years," Emily said with pointed teenage patience.

"My what?"

"You know, when we're all married and gone. We don't want to have to worry about you pining away all by yourself out here."

"Besides, you're still good-looking for your age," Ardeth contributed with a straight face. "Even Gary thinks you're sexy."

"Don't sound so amazed," B.J. muttered.

"Now, Mom, don't get all huffy on us. It's just that, well, we want you to be happy."

"I *am* happy."

Emily looked far from convinced. "Well, sure, but lately, you've been kinda uptight, you know? Like maybe you're, well, horny."

B.J. groaned inwardly, cursing the sexual revolution that allowed children to feel free discussing sex with their elders.

"Just for that, I'm going to take Ricky swimming." She shoved her dust rag into Emily's hands and stalked toward the door. "You two can finish up here without me."

Pausing outside to brush the dust from her jeans, she heard Ardeth say in a disgusted tone, "Way to go, Em."

"Hey, I'm just glad Mom seems interested in a guy again."

"Me, too, except, well, doesn't it bother you that she might get married again?"

"Not really. I mean, she hasn't had all that much luck with men, you know. Like, our biological father liked his job more than he liked being married, and then, just when everything is going great for her again, Dad gets killed. It's almost as if she's got this curse hanging over her or something."

B.J. heard Ardeth snort, and realized she'd been baldly eavesdropping. As she started to walk away, she heard Emily say firmly, "I still say she misses sex, and I think our new hired man is just the guy to make her admit it."

Four

Murdock parked B.J.'s truck in the same spot and retrieved his bags from the back. The stretch of grass between the house and outbuildings was deserted. Nothing was stirring, not even the leaves.

He'd spent half his life in places where a quiet like this would have had him keeping to cover, his weapon off safety, his finger on the trigger. But this was the good old US of A where folks hated terrorism and worshipped individual choice.

His mouth quirked at the thought.

The sun was still hot on his skin as he headed toward the grove and his temporary quarters. The place was a sniper's dream, he noted grimly. Plenty of cover in which to lie in wait, too many open spaces in which to catch a target unprotected and vulnerable, an unobstructed avenue of escape leading to the road.

He figured it could be worse—but not much.

The cabin door was wide open, as were all the windows. Somewhere inside, a guitar was being taken on a wild metallic ride at full volume. Whoever was listening had to be deaf or a teenager. Murdock put his money on the latter. Expecting Emily, he was surprised to find Ardeth instead.

She was sitting at the table by the window, bent over a magazine featuring glossy pictures of nearly naked women. Her face was in profile, but he noted her absorbed frown. At that same moment she spied the long stretch of his shadow on the bare floor and looked up.

He remembered an infant in pink blankets smelling of talcum. When he'd held her, she'd swatted at his nose with the tiniest hand he'd ever seen. And then she'd screamed bloody murder. He could still remember the panic he'd felt at that moment. The panic he *still* felt. Somehow he'd thought it would be easier than this to play the role of a stranger in his daughters' lives.

She started to speak, then realized the music was drowning out the sound of her voice and turned it down. "Whew, you scared the bejabbers out of me," she muttered, her face turning scarlet.

"Sorry." For a lot of things, none of which she needed to know.

"Uh, I'm Ardeth Dalton."

He nodded as though he hadn't known her as a baby with bananas in her hair and a toothless grin capable of melting concrete. As though he hadn't held her in his arms and felt an ache in his chest so strong he couldn't breathe.

"Cairn Murdock. I'm the new hired man."

"What happened to your hand?"

He glanced down at the handkerchief holding the split flesh together. By the time he'd reached the truck, he'd decided his hand wasn't broken. It just felt like it.

"Nothing serious."

He set his cases by the door and took a moment to check the place out. From where he stood he could see only one exit and too many windows without curtains, thrift-shop furniture and barracks-bare floors.

Dalton had to have been some kind of con artist to make B.J. think this place was romantic. Or, damn it, some kind of magician in the sack. That possibility had him silently, methodically, spewing out a long list of invective.

Ardeth watched warily, waiting until his eyes came to hers again before saying, "Uh, if you're looking for my mother, she isn't here. She took my little brother swimming."

"I thought that was Emily's job."

"It was, but me and her got into a hassle and Mom got fed up. She does sometimes, you know, and then she just goes off by herself to cool off. Mostly to this special spot she has in the woods, but sometimes, like today, she took Ricky to the river. They should be back soon, though. Mom likes to have dinner on the table before six."

The sun's angle said it was closer to five. "Place looks nice," he said as she continued to study him with intelligent, curious eyes. "Your work?"

"Mine and Mom's and my sister's." Her gaze dropped to the magazine she was trying to hide, and guilt crept into her face again. "I didn't buy it," she said a bit too quickly. "I found it on the shelf in the closet when I was dusting. Jack must've left it behind."

He walked to the table and glanced down. "December, 1993."

Her jaw dropped. "How did you know that?"

"For one thing Miss December there is wearing tinsel and for another, I remember reading it when I had a lot of time on my hands." Between bouts of dizziness and pain and a lot of flak from the nurses who had accused him of being politically incorrect.

"Seems to me there's not a lot to read," she muttered, and then giggled.

"Maybe you haven't gotten to the stories yet."

"I was curious is all." She aimed her stubborn little chin his way and dared him to criticize. So she had a temper like her mom, he mused. Him, he never let his emotions boil high enough to explode the way B.J.'s sometimes had.

"Find out anything interesting?"

She lifted one shoulder. "Actually I was trying to figure out how those women could even get into some of those poses. I mean, a person would have to be double-jointed or something, you know?"

Murdock nodded, his expression carefully solemn, but he felt an unexpected urge to laugh. "Or something," he agreed gravely.

"Anyway, I was just about finished when you showed up." Ardeth got to her feet and pushed back her hair. Her gaze shifted to his suitcases. "Is that all your stuff?"

"Everything but my truck, and I hired a pump jockey at the gas station to drive it out here after he gets off work. Big guy with red hair, looked to be about sixteen, seventeen. Said his name was Feller. Mike Feller, I think it was." He lifted his eyebrows and looked mildly interested. "Said he used to work for your mother."

"Did he also tell you Mom was the only one to give him a chance after he got out of youth camp?"

"Not that I recall."

"Well, she was! Just like she took on Pedro Gomez after he'd been fired off every other farm in the valley for drinking, and Jack, the guy who lived here, who wasn't real bright about a lot of things. Gary told me Jack couldn't even get hired on at the mill to sweep up." She stopped suddenly, a stricken look on her face. "I hate him," she muttered softly.

"Who? Jack?"

"No, Gary." Tears welled in her eyes, and she swallowed hard a couple of times. "He used to be my boyfriend—before his father turned him into a stupid coward."

The tears spilled past her lashes to run down her cheeks, and she dashed them away. "I'd better go," she said in a wavering voice. "So you can get settled and all."

Instead of leaving, however, she suddenly sank into her chair and buried her face in her hands. She sounded as though she were strangling on her sobs, and her small shoulders shook.

He'd seen her cry before—when she'd been wet or hungry or had a bellyache. Even as a novice father, he'd been able to figure out what to do to make the tears stop. And B.J. had always been there as backup. That thought had him looking west again, toward the river. He saw trees and clouds and the brown grass of midsummer. Nothing else.

What the hell did he do now?

Move, for one thing, he decided when he realized he'd all but rooted to the floor. His boots sounded too loud on the uncarpeted pine, and the scrape of the chair legs as he pulled it away from the table set his nerves on edge.

Ardeth looked up when he sat down, her face streaked with tears and her eyes already puffing. Murdock hadn't felt so helpless in years—not since B.J. had walked out, taking his children and a large chunk of his peace of mind with her.

He hooked his thumbs in his belt and pushed back until the chair balanced on two legs. "You want I should find this guy Gary and beat the living sh—hell out of him?"

Her eyes flashed. "Yes! No." She hiccuped. "I wish I'd never met him." Her words evoked another time, another place, only then it had been this girl's mother who had said them. About him.

"What seems to be the problem?"

"He said he loved me, and dumb me, I believed him!" Her mouth quivered again before she controlled it.

"Maybe he does. Maybe he's as miserable as you are."

"Ha!" She glared at him, her tears already drying. Anger was good, he thought. Even hate, if it crowded the sick, empty feeling out of a person's belly.

"I knew a guy once who was in the same kind of bind. Caught between the woman he loved and the compromises she wanted him to make. At the time he couldn't have both, so he had to make a choice. Damn near tore him in two making it."

Curiosity pushed some of the pain from her eyes. "What did he do?"

"He refused to bend, even for her, and then spent a lot of years trying to convince himself he'd made the right choice."

"Did it work?"

"No, but by the time he found that out it was too late." He eased the chair to four legs and stood. "I think I'll take a walk to the river and see if I can find your mom."

The path was well-worn and fairly steep, angling south-west. The sun was well along its path to the horizon, but the air was still hot, and the leaves hung limp and dusty on the branches over his head, waiting to be stirred by the night wind.

Rounding a bend, he caught his first whiff of the river. It was an earthy smell, one he liked. As a kid, he'd all but lived on the banks of a creek bordering his parents' property.

From the time they'd been old enough to see over the weeds, he and his buddies had ridden broomstick horses and killed Indians hidden in the rocks with cap guns. When they'd gotten older, they'd camped out under a railroad trestle and told ghost stories. He'd lost his virginity under that same trestle, and then felt oddly sad that his life would never be the same.

The path flattened and then flared into a rocky shelf that soon gave way to a sandy beach, where a sun-browned little boy was busily constructing an elaborate fort, complete with turrets and a moat.

B.J. was stretched out in a beach chair near a fallen log with her back to him, reading a book. Instead of dark glasses, she'd plopped a baseball cap on her head to shade her eyes. Instead of a bathing suit, she was wearing skimpy shorts and a faded tank top. She still had the best legs he'd ever seen—slim and sleek and sporting a lush tan.

He felt the sudden heat of sexual arousal start low in his belly and spread like wildfire. For an instant, control was beyond him. His mind, so disciplined in other things, ran straight and true to thoughts of steamy nights and cool sheets when her skin had been slick with passion, and those same golden thighs had opened to admit the eager thrusts of his all but bursting body.

He had only to close his eyes and he could see her again as she'd been on their wedding day, an angel in filmy white with so much love in her dark eyes he'd been bone-scared to touch her—and even more terrified to let her know how much he'd needed that love. Funny how dumb a guy could be—and how smart he could get when it was too late.

Wiping his face clean of all expression, he stepped forward, deliberately snapping a twig under his heel. She looked around quickly, her shoulders suddenly tense under the thin shirt. Once more, he noticed the shimmering sensuality that was as much a part of her as her Indian blood.

"Cairn! You startled me." Her voice was husky, her eyes drowsy as though she'd been lost in a daydream instead of the words on the page. Of him? he wondered, and then dismissed the idea as male conceit. If B.J. had sexual fantasies, he sure as hell wasn't included.

"Sorry. I just got back and figured you'd want to know."

"I appreciate that."

He stepped to the edge of the beach and, hands on hips, took a quick look-see at the surrounding area. The opposite bank was head high and covered with brambles in an unbroken line to a small spit jutting into the water. A narrow deer path led from the trees above to the shore.

Focusing on the water, he figured it to be four or five feet deep in the center, tapering to inches on either side. No trouble at all to cross—if that were a man's intention. Ahead was a sharp bend and the faint sound of water rippling over an obstruction of some kind.

"What's in the shack?" he asked, indicating a small, weathered shed to his left, standing a good ten feet from the water's edge.

"That's the pump house. You can't see from here, but there's an intake pipe sunk in the river right behind it."

"You irrigate from the river?"

"Yes. Everyone with river frontage does."

Mentally marking the place as a potential ambush blind, he turned to find the boy standing by his mother's chair, staring at him with B.J.'s big brown eyes. An irrational anger at the man who'd given her this child ran through him before he fought it down. Like jealousy, it was a useless waste of a man's time.

"Uh, hi there, buddy." He'd gathered his share of stares over the years, but none were quite as intense as a curious child's.

The kid frowned. "Mommy, who's that man?"

"That's Mr. Murdock, sweet stuff. He's taking Jack's place. And this is Ricky, the man of the Dalton family." She lifted her gaze to Murdock's, and he saw the pride in her face.

He'd been in the company of admirals, and even a president or two. There wasn't a reason in the world he should find himself ill at ease, even worried that the kid wouldn't like him.

"Glad to meet you, Ricky."

The boy's eyebrows formed a puzzled line over a small, freckled nose. "How come he looks so grumpy?"

B.J. looked surprised at the question, and then her lips curved. "Why don't you ask him?"

Ricky ducked his head, suddenly shy. "Uh-uh. You ask him."

Her gaze fixed on Murdock's once more. "My son would like to know why you look so grumpy."

What guy wouldn't when he was faced with an ex-wife who'd gotten sexier over the years and a little boy that might have been his if he hadn't screwed up big-time?

"I missed lunch," he said, forcing a smile for the boy. "I always look grumpy when my belly's empty."

"There you go, Rick, Mr. Murdock gets in a bad mood when he's hungry." She grinned at her son. "Just like another male I know around these parts." She poked a gentle finger into his chubby tummy and Ricky giggled as he shied away.

"No tickling, Mommy," he chided, his eyes bright with expectation.

"Oops, I forgot tickling's only for babies, not big boys."

Murdock dropped his gaze to the ground and tried to force his mind away from the image of B.J.'s mischievous grin right before she'd bent to brush tickling little nips down the arrow of hair on his belly. She'd called him her big boy, too.

He'd bedded willing women after the divorce, some just to prove to himself he still could, but none had had B.J.'s knack of making him enjoy sex for more than the physical release it could bring.

As he leaned over to pick up a rock, he told himself he didn't miss it. Palming the smooth chunk of granite, feeling its weight, its warm surface, he told himself he couldn't turn back the clock. With a grunt, he flung the stone toward the opposite bank and told himself he didn't feel more for this woman than responsibility.

"Nice shot," B.J. muttered when the stone flushed a trio of jays from a tangle of brambles. Their raucous scolding echoed over the water, shattering the tranquillity.

"Mommy, I have to go potty," Ricky piped in the midst of the racket.

"Then you'd better run, sweets. And don't forget to flush."

"I won't." The youngster threw a last curious look Murdock's way, then took off running up the path barefoot.

Murdock winced at the thought of the sharp stones and thorny twigs underfoot, and then realized that little boys were immune to mortal discomfort, especially in summer when the days were long and full of things to see and do.

He pushed his fingertips into his back pockets and watched a dragonfly impatiently investigating a lacy white flower growing along the path.

"Cute kid," he said, moving suddenly tense shoulders. "Bet he keeps you busy."

"Especially in the summer."

He turned in time to see her closing her book and preparing to stand. Southern-bred habits were hard to break, and he had his hand extended to help before she looked up.

Watching her eyes, he saw her hesitate. Ignoring him would be bad manners. But accepting his offer would be tacitly acceding to age-old rules of gender she professed to hate so much.

"It's a hell of a dilemma, isn't it?"

She scowled, then slowly her eyes twinkled and her mouth relaxed into a rueful smile as she slipped her hand into his. Her fingers were slender, her bones delicate under the tanned skin, but her small palm was ridged with calluses that hadn't been there twelve years ago.

"I used to hate it when you read my mind," she admitted as she let him pull her to her feet. A quick tug and she'd be in his arms, her soft breasts warming his chest. He savored the thought before releasing her. For good measure he took a step backward.

"I didn't read your mind, only your face. With most people there's a difference, but not with you."

She regarded him curiously. "No?"

He shook his head. "It's your eyes mostly. Like now, you're wondering if you should ask me to dinner tonight."

Her jaw dropped. "How did—I was not!" Even as she protested, her face was turning pink along the rise of her cheekbones, and he had to work at his poker face.

"Actually I was wondering if I should offer to lend you some staples so that you could make your *own* dinner."

"Ah, a subtle difference, I agree."

"Don't look so smug. Don't forget I'm the boss around here." Her lips curved into the friendliest smile he'd gotten from her so far.

He glanced toward the slippery sheen of brown river midstream and wondered if the water was cold enough to ice down the raging heat in his veins.

"Ready?" he asked, restless now, and far too aware of the dangerous line he was walking.

"Yes, the sun will be gone soon." She reached for the chair and so did he. Their hands touched. She recoiled. He froze.

"You're hurt," she murmured, staring in horror at the stain of blood on the white handkerchief.

"Not much."

"What happened?"

He shrugged. "Sarge and I had a talk."

"You hit him?"

"Let's say I had a point to make and I made it the quickest way I knew how."

"What point?"

"That I'd just quit the mill and hired on here. I figured he'd spread the word that you weren't in this all alone."

An old forgotten ache started pulsing inside her again. She should be angry at his presumption, appalled at the violence. Instead she felt . . . touched.

"Once a SEAL, always a SEAL," she said softly.

"Guess so." His mouth still gentled right before he smiled. And her heart still pounded when his mouth hovered over hers.

"We'd better go."

"Not yet." His brows were drawn as though he were in great pain, and his gaze was trained on her mouth.

"Cairn, don't." Even as she spoke, she found her pulse starting to gallop and her mouth going dry.

"Don't what?" His voice was pitched low, like a strained whisper in the dark. "Don't remember what it feels like to kiss you? Don't wake up at night sometimes and want you like hell, even after all these years?"

"We can't—"

His mouth smothered the rest, no longer gentle.

If she had stiffened, he might have pulled back. Maybe.

If she'd resisted in any way, he would have been satisfied with a taste. Perhaps.

But she did neither, and that surprised them both.

While his mouth took hers again and again, the blood pounded in her head and a moan rose in her throat. His mouth stilled, then slowly parted. His tongue played over her lips, leaving them moist and hot. Faint at first, desire suddenly ran like wildfire through her, taking all the air from her lungs. She shuddered, her body beyond her rational need to resist.

His arms came around her, solid and warm and thick with layered muscle that could turn to steel at his bidding. Hard fingers splayed against the curve of her spine, lifting her without effort until she was balanced on tiptoes. One hand came up to cup her chin, while his tongue mated with hers.

Already shaky, her knees turned weak, and a low, heady thrumming began deep inside her. Instantly, as though sensing her mind's surrender to her body, his arms gentled even as his mouth found the throbbing pulse in her throat.

His tongue teased, his mouth tasted.

He had no right to remember, she thought through a haze of rising pleasure. No right to tempt her this way. And yet, the wanting had been in her, lying dormant, waiting.

Now it swirled through her like smoke and silk, leaving her skin tingling and her nerves singing. She felt light-headed, drenched in sweetness, and then, as he abruptly broke contract, dazed.

She swayed, hands clinging to his shirt for support. Her eyes opened in slow motion, her breathing a rush of sound. He was looking at her with eyes nearly as dark as her own now, and his lean, hard face had the taut, tense look of frustrated arousal.

"Now you know. I still want you, Barbara Jane. Probably always will, which is my own particular kind of hell." He traced the shocked curve of her mouth with his fingertip, and a look she found unsettling came into his eyes, adding potency to the lone-wolf strength of his rugged features.

She raised shaking fingers to her mussed hair and tried to repair the damage. It wouldn't do for the children to see her disheveled and flushed, especially the girls, who were already attributing her recent mood swings to sexual frustration.

"This shouldn't have happened. I…it can't happen again. I mean it, Cairn."

He heard the words and saw the passion in her face. Wild and hungry, it matched his own. He knew he'd never rest until he'd had her again, one last time. But now was not the time, nor did he intend to take what he needed her to give willingly.

"But it did happen, sweetheart. Likely it will again."

Something akin to panic flared in her eyes, and she shook her head. "No, we can be friends, but nothing more. I want your word on that."

His grin flashed, more comfortable now. "No way, sweetheart. But I'll back off for now. Besides, it's almost six, and your kids expect dinner."

He retrieved her chair, then stepped back politely to let her precede him. Still shaken and not at all sure she'd won more than a brief truce, she squared her shoulders and started up the path. At the top, he paused.

"One more thing," he said when she turned to see why he'd stopped. "That pump house is perfect for a sniper to lie in wait, so until further notice, this place is off-limits."

Five

B.J. tucked her grocery list in her purse and headed for the truck. Normally she enjoyed her trips into town and always gave herself extra time to visit with Ruth Walker at the town's one and only boutique and dry-goods store, or share a cup of coffee and the latest gossip with Marlene First at the Tip Top Café. Both women had been friends since high school, and she would have bet big money they'd stick by her, no matter what.

She would have lost that same big money. Ruthie's sister was Garson Tremaine's secretary, and Marlene's husband drove a log truck for Cascade. Neither woman was willing to risk a family disaster just to remain her friend.

Such things hurt. They no longer surprised her.

In the three weeks since the picnic, her usual day-to-day problems had gone from annoying to downright epidemic. Her tractor had developed an oil leak and no one in town seemed to have time to fix it, not even the Farley brothers, who had been maintaining Berryman equipment since her grandfather's time. And the company that had trucked her fruit to the warehouse in Medford for the past three seasons had suddenly run into a shortage of drivers willing to haul for Berryman Farm.

Closer to home, her children were treating Cairn more like a member of the family than a hired hand. In fact, Ardeth and Emily seemed to go out of their way to ask his advice about clothes and boys and hairstyles.

Did he like long hair or short better? Did he like tall women or short? Slim or "stacked"? Which perfume did he like best? How come boys never seemed to like the girls who liked them first? What did he think of the feminist movement? Birth control? Sexual freedom?

To his credit, he was supremely patient with them, answering each and every question with a serious reflection that seemed completely genuine. Not only that, he seemed almost touchingly pleased when they seemed so eager to spend time with him.

True to her promise, B.J. did nothing to discourage their fondness, nor his. Nor did she worry that he would slip and tell them who he was, although she did worry constantly about their reaction when he left.

At least twice a week they'd come up with urgent reasons why he should be invited to dinner. Once it was because he was already in the kitchen, fixing the drip under the sink, when dinnertime rolled around.

Another time, it was to get a man's opinion on a recipe for beef stew Emily had found in an old recipe book while rummaging through the attic on one of her whimsical "treasure" hunts among the old trunks and boxes stored there. He'd given his approval by eating three helpings and then complimenting the chef with the savoir faire of the officer and gentleman he'd been.

As for Ricky, his shyness had lasted exactly two days— until Cairn had shown him how to whistle piercingly through his teeth. In the largely unfathomable world of little boys that was apparently a prized skill, and the louder the better, and one that B.J. had never mastered and, therefore, hadn't been able to teach her poor, underprivileged son.

Worst of all, she herself had taken to thinking of Cairn at odd moments during the day and then dreaming of him in-

stead of Roger at night. So far she had managed to avoid
being alone with Cairn, but it disturbed her greatly that she
couldn't seem to shove the memory of his kiss out of her
mind.

Perhaps a new lipstick would help, she decided, pulling
her keys from her bag. Or maybe she'd splurge on a whole
new outfit. Something bright and cheery and terribly self-
indulgent.

Yes, that was the ticket. She just needed to pamper herself more, and then she would stop craving the wrong man's
touch when she was lying alone in her bed with the moonlight shining through the window and her skin burning beneath the thin sheet.

"Going somewhere, boss?"

Startled, B.J. spun around to find Murdock heading her
way. From the looks of the mud on his logging boots and the
water stains on his shirt and jeans, he'd been wrestling with
the irrigation system again.

For a man who had worn a starched dress uniform complete with sword and medals as though born to the formal
traditions it exemplified, he seemed surprisingly at ease
covered with grime and a farmhand's sweat.

A dozen times a day she reminded herself that she was
definitely not impressed by rock hard shoulders a mile wide
and a lean wedge of masculine torso. Nor was she particularly susceptible to tight jeans on a man or the corded muscles packed into that same straining denim.

Well, once maybe. When she'd been fresh from the sticks
and wild to try new things. But not now. Now she was a
mother of three, pushing forty faster than she cared to admit, and far more sensible. Character counted with her more
than sex appeal in a man. Staying power and steadiness were
more important than the kind of raw masculine looks her
girls called "prime."

But her throat still went dry whenever Murdock came into
view. And her heart still sped. That was bad enough. Much
to her discomfort, she couldn't seem to find much wrong
with his character these days, either, so every time she saw
him she'd taken to reminding herself that he would soon be
leaving.

"I'm going into town to do some shopping. Do you need anything?"

"About a thousand feet of new pipe and a new timer for the pump, but I'll settle for two dozen new gaskets." He pulled a red bandanna from his back pocket and swabbed his damp face. Since he'd started working the fields for her, his forearms had taken on an added layer of bronze that made the soft brown hair on his arms seem almost white in contrast.

"What kind of gaskets?"

"This kind." He exchanged the handkerchief for a worn circle of dusty rubber he'd evidently stuffed into the same back pocket.

She took it from him, her fingers brushing his. From the looks of it, the irrigation valves were in worse shape than she'd figured. No wonder they were losing pressure to the sprinkler heads.

"If I remember correctly, Roger used to get these at Grady's Hardware. We have a charge there." She frowned. "Well, we used to, anyway. These days..." She let the thought hang. There was no reason to finish it.

"You're good for it, aren't you?" His tone had an edge.

"Of course! Well, after the crop is sold, I am."

"Then there's no problem."

"Maybe not for you, but there might be for Sam Grady. Cascade throws a lot of business his way, much more than I do."

He shrugged. "I'll have a talk with him."

He took her elbow and steered her toward the shade where her truck sat side by side with his. His grip was firm enough to control but not cause pain. The physical kind, anyway. "We'll take my truck. It's not as well-known around town."

"There's no need for you to go with me," she said when they reached the trucks.

"Matter of opinion." He opened the door and nodded toward the dark interior. "Slide in."

B.J. glared at him. "I am not one of your men, Commander. Stop giving me orders."

"Ex-commander. And consider it a request if it makes you happier."

"It doesn't."

Temper was building in her eyes again, and satisfaction moved through him. As long as she was mad at him, she wouldn't have time to notice the hard anger building against her around town.

"Look, if you're ticked off because I kissed you—"

"I'm not ticked off," she shot back, her eyes shooting sparks. "I'm hassled, and I'm tired, and I'm fed up feeling like a prisoner on my own land."

So that was it. He had expected flak when he'd laid down a few commonsense rules, and now he was getting it. Like most things, he figured it was better to meet it head-on.

"Hassled and tired, I can understand." He kept his tone low and steady. "But the other...you're not a prisoner and you know it."

"What would you call it then?"

"Prudence."

Her scowl deepened to a tempting pout. "I can't even take a walk without you tagging along."

"I just don't want you wandering around alone, especially in the woods."

"I like being alone in the woods. That's the point."

"So I'll stay behind a tree. Believe me, you won't even know I'm there."

Wrong. She had developed an odd sixth sense about him. For instance, she knew that he suffered from frequent headaches, and that he never went into the sun without a hat or sunglasses shading his eyes. And that he sometimes staggered when he was particularly tired.

She'd asked him very casually one day if the injury that had beached him was still giving him trouble and had gotten a cold warning to back off on the Florence Nightingale routine.

She'd also noticed that he conducted a kind of patrol every night before he turned in, walking the perimeter of the house and yard as though tucking them all in safely before he allowed himself to rest.

"Now listen to me, Cairn. I'm the Berryman in Berryman Farm, which, as you persist in calling me, makes me the boss. Right now, the boss is going to town, and she doesn't need a bodyguard."

Letting the cynical smile she'd always hated play over his mouth, he dug into his watch pocket and pulled out his lucky silver dollar. "I'll flip, you call. Heads you go alone, tails I go with you."

She stared at the coin in his hand. "You're joking, right?"

Eyes locked on hers, he tossed the coin into the air and let it fall into the dust. Instinct had her glancing down, but he'd already covered the dollar with his muddy boot.

"Heads or tails?" His tone was soft silk, with just enough steel licking the edges to set her teeth on edge.

"Heads."

"You're sure about that?"

She drew a quick breath and glared. "Yes, I'm sure," she said through a tight jaw.

"Aye, aye." He stepped back, and she looked down.

"Tails," she muttered. "Damn."

"Tough luck." He bent to retrieve his coin, only to have her beat him to it.

"Just a minute." She examined the dollar closely, emotion building in her chest. Minted in the year Murdock had been born, she'd given it to him on their wedding night. As long as he carried it with him, she'd told him, he would always come back to her.

The first time he'd left on a mission she'd found it in his drawer under his socks. She'd been crushed—until she'd discovered that her new husband was frequently sent places where he could be summarily shot if he was captured carrying anything bearing the stamp of the United States of America.

"I'm surprised you kept it."

"After the divorce, I thought about throwing it in the Potomac."

"Why didn't you?"

His shrug was more reflex than emotion. Why had she expected more? "Just never got around to it, I guess." So much for sentiment.

He took the dollar from her hand and returned it to his pocket. "Ready?" His drawl was just a touch too smug to be ignored.

"Do you know something, Murdock? I really, *really* wish you hadn't left the Navy, because if you hadn't, you'd be off in some hellhole or another on one of your precious missions, having a great time harassing someone else." Glowering, she sidestepped the open door to his truck and headed for her own.

"Hey, not so fast."

He caught up with her before she'd managed three steps and swung her around. "What now?" she demanded hotly.

He took a fast look around, then bent forward and gave her a quick, hard kiss.

"Don't look so shocked, B.J. That was just to seal our deal."

"*Your* deal, Murdock. I'm an unwilling participant."

"Duly noted." His mouth softened. "Maybe we'd better practice that a few more times, though—just until you stop looking like you want to murder me."

"There's no 'like' about it. I *do* want to murder you." She wrenched open the door to her truck and hopped into the seat. She had already started the engine and was shifting into first by the time he jumped into the seat next to her.

She counted it a major victory that neither one spoke all the way into town.

Hayden Tremaine was as much a legend as a businessman. Orphaned at fourteen, with little more than a spare shirt and a secondhand pair of logging boots to his name, he'd talked his way onto a logging crew near Roseburg for fifty cents a day and food.

That had been seventy years ago, when loggers used mules and oxen and crosscut saws taller than most men. In those days a man who worked hard and saved his money had a chance to make it big in the Northwest. Now he owned two mills and a good part of the county.

Officially retired, although he'd prudently kept a seat on Cascade's board, he devoted as much energy and care to fishing as he'd once devoted to building a logging empire.

On those days when he found time to visit one or the other of his mills, he preferred to roam the steamy, noisy caverns where the logs were processed into lumber instead of the boardroom.

So when he showed up in Garson's office at Mill Number One on a gloomy Friday morning at the end of July, the younger man didn't bother to hide his surprise.

Respectful as always, he shot to his feet and then stood awkwardly behind his desk. No matter how old he got or how many deals he closed, his father still had the power to reduce him to an insecure kid with a simple lifting of one eyebrow.

"Fish not biting today, Pop?"

"Maybe they are, maybe they're not. Haven't taken the boat out to find out."

The elder Tremaine strolled to the window overlooking the yard. His carriage was still as erect as a strapping boy of fourteen, but his eyes had grown dim with age and his hearing required mechanical aids, which he hated.

"Been visiting with the men?" Garson asked, coming up behind his father to share the view.

Hayden grunted an assent. "Hear you had a run-in with Noah's daughter at the company picnic."

"We had a public discussion, you might say, yes."

"Some say she stood up to you pretty good. Said something about greedy mill owners, I hear."

Garson shot a disgusted look toward the mountain range beyond the mill yard. Berryman land was out there in that green swath of pine and fir covering the mountaintop. Enough board feet to keep the mill's profits steady for at least a year.

"You know B.J., Pop. She's always had a mouth on her."

Hayden turned to regard his only son with eyes that still saw more than he let on. "There was a time I hoped she might become my daughter-in-law."

Garson bit down on a curse. "That was twenty years ago, Pop. Puppy love."

The old man's eyebrows arched upward. At first glance his expression seemed benign, perhaps even a bit simple-minded—unless a person chanced to notice the telltale glint of a brilliant intelligence in those watery eyes.

"Hmm, I seem to recall you asking your mama for grandma's ring. Told her you were planning to marry the girl as soon as she graduated high school. 'Course I could be wrong about that. My memory's not as good as it was when I was your age."

Garson returned to his chair and sat down. "It's good enough," he said with a grudging smile. "Truth is, she turned me down flat. Seems she had these big plans, you know? Had this scholarship to Oregon State and then she was going to get away from the Northwest. For good, she said."

"Women have been known to change their minds. Your mama did."

"Yeah, but you had to go all the way to France to bring her back."

Hayden's face softened as it always did when he spoke of his late wife. "It took some persuading. Darn near six months. Got so sick of red wine and rich food I would've killed for a bloody steak and a bottle of beer."

"Mama told me you lost twenty pounds and she felt so sorry for you she decided to marry you so she wouldn't have your death on her conscience."

Hayden chuckled. "She never let me forget it, either. Especially when I got her back up about something or other." He drew a shaky breath. "Damn, but I miss that woman."

Garson thought about his own two marriages, both of which had ended in messy—and costly—divorces. "Mama always liked B.J."

"Could be that's something you've forgotten."

Garson reached for a cigarette from the pack on his desk. Ignoring his father's sudden frown, he lighted it with a monogrammed gold lighter and blew smoke toward the ceiling.

"Those things will kill you, son."

"I'm going to quit—just as soon as the pressure eases enough."

Hayden pulled out a chair and sat down slowly, giving his arthritic limbs time to settle. "Wasn't but a month ago you claimed you and B.J. were close to signing a timber lease. Seems to me that should ease the pressure considerably."

"She'll sign."

His father's eyebrows lifted higher this time. "I'm hearing different."

"She's stubborn, but she's not stupid. Once she understands how deep the resentment in these parts is running against her, she'll, ah, readjust her priorities."

His father snorted. "Sounds like you miscalculated."

"She has this thing about those damn trees. Claims they're sacred or some such nonsense."

"Just like her father. Old Noah, now there was stubborn for you. The man could have been a millionaire twice over if he'd agreed to trade those trees of his for a share in my first mill."

Garson stifled a sigh. He'd heard all of his father's stories many times. Privately, he considered Noah Berryman a fool of the first order. Voicing that opinion, however, would have only gotten his father's back up, something Garson couldn't risk. Not when Hayden was already questioning his decision to step aside and turn things over to his son.

"Look, Pop, I know you were fond of the old man, and damn near everyone in the county knows you were disappointed when B.J. and I didn't end up together like you and Noah always planned, but times are different now, and we need those trees. Otherwise, we'll have to shut down one shift for sure at both mills, maybe two. And if the government doesn't stop diddling around, we just might have to close down Number Two altogether."

Garson took a deep drag on his cigarette, puffing out smoke impatiently. "I can't let that happen, Pop. Whatever I have to do, I'll do."

Hayden's gaze sharpened suddenly, as though he'd pulled himself back from some pleasant reverie. "I agree."

"Then why—"

"I don't want her hurt."

Garson kept the relief from his tone and the triumph from his expression. "C'mon, Pop. You can't really believe I'd authorize anything more dangerous than a little psychological warfare."

"I hear she's got a new hired man. Someone who used to work at Number One. Someone tough enough—or foolhardy enough—to have walked into the Junction and decked Sarge Crookshank for making an off-color remark about her."

Garson shrugged. "Some logger with a crush. I'm not worried."

"Maybe you should be."

Garson took a long drag on his cigarette and watched his father through the smoke he exhaled. Scowling, Hayden waved the smoke away from his face.

"I talked to Gary. He told me you laid down the law to him about not dating B.J.'s oldest girl."

"All part of the plan. That and a general boycott of workers. When the chips are down, hit 'em where it hurts most. Isn't that what you always told me?" He took a last pull on his cigarette, then put it out in a tray that was already half full. "In this case it's the farm itself. When B.J. realizes she's about to lose more than a few trees, she'll come around, I guarantee it."

Hayden stared into his son's eyes for a long time. Garson had to dig deep to keep his true feelings from showing. The old man had gotten mellow in his old age, but he'd been as ruthless in his day as anyone. More, if the stories he'd heard about Hayden's strikebreaking tactics in the thirties were true. Four men had died and scores had been injured before the mill owners had succeeded in keeping the unions out of the valley.

"I want your word, Garson. No rough stuff."

"Leave it to me, Pop," he said in his most persuasive tone. "I don't intend to do anything you wouldn't do if you were still sitting in this chair."

Murdock wiped his greasy hands on the rag Ricky handed him and grunted his satisfaction.

"Is it fixed now, Cairn?" Ricky asked, his button eyes bright with interest.

"Should be, but a good mechanic never leaves anything to chance."

"Why not?"

"Because equipment is a lot like some people. You think you know what's going to happen and why, but you can't ever be sure until you check it out, which is why you and I are going to take this baby for a test drive before I let your mom have it back."

"Can I steer?"

"Don't you always?"

"Not always. Only when I'm with you. Mommy says I'm too little." Ricky scrambled onto the back hitch, then waited for Cairn to settle into the seat before climbing onto his lap.

B.J. was mending a broken door on the equipment shed, and the girls were cleaning house, so Ricky had become his charge for the afternoon.

"How do you check out people?" he asked as Murdock reached around him to pull out the throttle. He was used to Ricky's abundant supply of questions, just as he was accustomed to Emily's bluntness and Ardeth's moods. B.J. was the one who kept him guessing.

"You check out people the same way you check out tractors."

"You can't drive people!"

"No, but you can watch how they operate."

"How?"

"Watch how they look at you, listen to what they say. Ask questions and pay attention to the way they answer." He put the lever into neutral, shoved in the clutch and turned the key. The motor turned over with satisfying ease, then settled into the distinctive rhythm of a diesel engine.

"Is that why you're always watching Mommy when she's not looking?" Ricky asked over the rumble. "To check her out?"

"Something like that."

The kid was quick. Murdock made a mental note to watch himself when Ricky was around. One more thing to keep in mind, like pretending the girls' problems were someone else's responsibility and telling himself a dozen times a day that he was just the hired hand and B.J. was just his boss.

He did the shifting while Ricky steered. After a rocky start and a lot of patience on Murdock's part, the boy had learned to keep the tractor moving in a relatively straight line.

"There's Mommy!" the boy cried when he spied his mother working on the door to the shed. "Let's show her how good I can drive, okay?"

"Okay."

Turning was a skill Rick had yet to master, so Murdock covered the boy's small hands with his and gently guided the tractor to the right. When they were headed straight again, he let the boy handle things on his own, just as he'd let the girls recruit him into refereeing their sisterly squabbles and commandeering his cabin when they wanted to play the music their mother hated.

It wasn't as if he was a real member of the family, he told himself daily to ease his conscience. From the first day he'd made it a point to remind the kids that his stay at Berryman Farm was only temporary. More in the nature of a favor until the furor over the trees died down was the way he'd put it.

A father he wasn't. He knew it, they knew it. Still, whenever one of the kids called him "Cairn," he wondered what it would feel like to be called "Dad."

Dealing with B.J. was a whole different set of headaches. Part of the problem was the weather. Since it had turned hot, she'd taken to wearing shorts instead of jeans.

At the moment she was bending over, attaching a metal brace to the bottom of the shed door, her fanny swaying seductively with each blow of her hammer. The feeling that hit him was hot and hard and below the belt. It moved through him like a building wave, gaining speed as it moved. Steeling himself, he rode out the curl.

Hearing the tractor approach, she tapped one last nail in place, then slowly straightened, stretching her back and her neck to work out the kinks.

The weather had turned steamy as well as hot, and her thin knitted shirt was damp from her exposed throat to a ragged spot between her breasts. Groaning silently, Cairn resolved to keep his gaze on her face or the shed or any damned place but the tempting, almost naked curves.

"Look at me, Mommy, I'm driving!" Ricky called as Murdock throttled back the engine to an idle before turning it off.

"So I see."

She wiped her face with the back of her work glove, leaving a smudge of dust on one cheek. Beneath the brim of her baseball cap, her gaze skimmed Murdock's face before settling on her son's. "Looks like you're going to need a good scrubbing to clean off all the grease, too."

B.J. ignored the sheepish look on Cairn's face, just as she ignored the sexy picture he made in tight jeans and a chest-hugging shirt with rolled sleeves.

"Cairn fixed the place that was leaking, and I helped."

"You did? How about that!"

Ricky beamed, so proud he was all but bouncing up and down on Cairn's lap. It was on the tip of her tongue to order him to be careful when she noticed the subtle way Cairn framed the boy with his arms, keeping him safe without destroying Ricky's growing sense of pride.

A pressure built in her chest until it was difficult to breathe properly. Whether he would ever admit it or not, Cairn would have made a wonderful father.

"Ricky, sweetie, will you please run in the house and get me a soda from the fridge?"

His expression turned cagey. "Can I have one, too?"

"Okay, but just one."

"Yaah!" Ricky cheered.

With a movement so smooth it seemed effortless, Murdock curled one arm around Ricky's waist and lowered him to the side of the tractor, well clear of the big wheel. Ricky's sneakers were already moving when they hit the ground.

Murdock watched him go, an absorbed, almost pained look around his hard mouth. "Kid has more energy than he knows what to do with."

"If he gets to be a pest, don't hesitate to say so. Babysitting isn't really part of your job."

"He's not much trouble. Besides, I like the company." He removed his hat and hung it on the gear lever before measuring the sun's angle with narrowed eyes. An instant later, he slipped on the aviator sunglasses he invariably carried in his shirt pocket. "Want me to finish that for you?"

B.J. thought about her aching back and the paperwork still to be done. "If you don't mind."

"You're the boss. I'll just put your hot rod in the shed first."

He was reaching for the key again when he caught sight of movement to his left. He shifted focus too quickly, and paid for it with a sudden stab of pain behind his right eye.

"What the hell?"

He glowered at the two girls sauntering toward them from the direction of the river. Both were wearing bathing suits and carrying towels and beach chairs.

He mouthed a vicious curse before giving B.J. the kind of look he generally reserved for screwups.

"Don't start, Cairn. I gave them permission."

He liked a challenge as well as the next man, he thought, climbing from the seat. If he had the time, he would have relished the give-and-take involved with curbing that mile wide streak of independence she'd cultivated since they split. But time was the one thing in short supply right now. That and patience.

"Care to tell me why?" He kept his voice low, his gaze fixed on those simmering brown eyes.

"It's hot, the girls were bored and none of their friends have called in weeks. They needed a diversion."

He had to admire her guts. He was also ready to strangle her with his bare hands. "I give up," he muttered. "Go ahead and stick your head in the sand."

The grinding ache that usually waited until sometime after midnight to settle behind his eyes was starting early and getting stronger beat by beat. What was it Frundt had said when he'd left Bethesda? Avoid stress? He'd like to see Frundt or any other man try that around B.J. Berryman.

"Hi," Ardeth said brightly as the girls approached. "Isn't it a gorgeous day?"

Murdock figured it was anything but, and said so.

B.J. shot him a murderous look before regarding her daughter in amazement. "Is this the same girl who was talking about taking holy orders and living in a cloister the rest of her life?"

Emily rolled her eyes. "Guess who was down by the swimming hole?"

B.J. saw Cairn stiffen. "Suppose you save time and tell us," he ordered in a harder than necessary tone.

Emily flashed him a forgiving smile. "Gary-the-Wimp Tremaine."

Ardeth drew a sharp breath. "That's not fair, Em. You heard him apologize."

"I heard him trying to weasel out of taking you to the fair next month, too."

"It's just that his father would be upset, and—"

"See, what'd I tell you? A wimp." Emily directed her comment to Cairn, as though the two of them were somehow in cahoots.

"You're just jealous," Ardeth declared, her chin taking a haughty angle.

"Of you and Gary? No way."

"Brat." Ardeth stalked off, her thongs slapping the dusty ground with each step.

B.J. sighed. "Your sister's right, Em. You are a brat sometimes."

"Yeah, I know, but sometimes I think Ardie needs a keeper. Like now." She batted a persistent fly away from her sunburned nose and managed a scowl at the same time. "That jerk Gary all but admitted his father was out to get you, and Ardie just smiled and nodded and acted like she didn't care if we got thrown off our land or not, just as long as she and Gary didn't have to break up over it."

B.J. saw Cairn's jaw set and could have crowned her middle child with the handiest object, which just happened to be a ratty beach chair that had seen better days. "Now, Em—" she began, only to have Cairn's raspy voice interrupt.

"What—exactly—did Gary-the-Wimp say?"

"Mostly dumb stuff about Ardie and him being caught in the middle and how he didn't care what Mom did with her trees."

"Anything else?"

Emily drew her eyebrows together over eyes that were suddenly deep in thought. "He did say that Mr. Tremaine nearly had a stroke when he found out Mr. Grady had sold us pipes and things on credit. Made him come to the mill and then called him all kinds of names. Gary said his dad has sworn to get our trees, no matter whose head he had to bash in to get 'em.''

"Mom, did you say Ricky could take two pops from the fridge?''

Turning, she saw Ardeth holding open the screen door to the back porch. "Yes," she shouted back. "Why?"

"Don't worry, I'll help him clean up the mess." Ardeth disappeared and the screen door banged shut.

"Oh Lord. What next?"

"Don't look at me," Emily said, moving off. "I have to wash river germs out of my hair before it turns green."

"It's also your night to start dinner," B.J. called after her. "The menu's on the fridge."

B.J. steeled herself for the gloating look she expected from Cairn. Instead he seemed preoccupied, almost dazed. A closer look had her frowning to herself. He had another headache, and from the tension already framing his mouth, this one was bad.

"Cairn—"

"Leave the hammer. I'll fix the door later. Right now, it's too hot to work." He turned and walked off.

Toward the river.

The boy was built along lean lines, with the oversize hands and feet of an adolescent rocketing toward adulthood. Still in swim trunks, he was standing at the river's edge, staring at the splash of sun on the surface. His shoulders were hunched, his hands fisted on his hips, the picture of a kid in trouble trying to think his way out.

Murdock scanned the area quickly, saw nothing worth worrying about, and allowed himself a moment to collect his thoughts before calling a greeting.

The boy whirled, defiance already in his eyes. "What the—who the hell are you?"

"Hired help. Name's Murdock."

"Ardie said her mom hired a new guy. Guess that's you."

Murdock inclined his head slowly. "You got a name?"

"Tremaine. Gary Tremaine, if that makes a difference." The look on his face said it should.

Murdock had seen his share of kids like this over the years. A bit pampered, a lot spoiled. Intelligent, but cocky and inclined to resist authority—traits that weren't necessarily all that bad, if a man knew how to direct them. And he did.

"Names don't mean diddly, son. The fact you're trespassing on private property does."

Surprise flared in the boy's blue eyes, followed by a wash of anger. "My family can buy and sell this place, buddy."

"Until they do, you're still trespassing. Question is, why?"

"None of your business."

Amused, Murdock nevertheless refrained from cracking a smile. The kid had guts, even if he didn't have much street sense.

"Wrong, ace. Anything that causes trouble around here is very much my business." Cruelly, deliberately, he put twenty years of command experience into his tone, and watched the boy's eyes fill with sudden alarm. He didn't like using muscle on the kid—or anyone. Sometimes it was the only way.

Tremaine Junior's gaze went to a spot across the river, and Murdock could almost hear the wheels grind in the kid's head. A glint of red metal through the dense foliage told Murdock the kid had gotten past him by four-wheeling through the woods, and he made a note to check out the other bank.

"Trust me, kid. You'll never make it." Murdock shoved his hands in his pockets and ambled forward, a deceptively bland smile playing over his mouth. He'd given the kid the stick. Now it was time for the carrot. "And I do know who you are, Gary. Ardeth has mentioned your name more than one since I hired on."

The boy was still wary, but the hot-wired panic was ebbing. "Me and her, we're friends, sort of—or we were until my old man got a burr up his butt. Now..." He shrugged. "I'm supposed to forget I even knew her."

Murdock lifted his eyebrows. "Seems like you don't take orders all that well."

Gary frowned. "Don't get me wrong, my dad's a good guy and all, but he has this thing about Ardie's mom and those stupid trees of hers."

"What kind of 'thing' is that?"

"You know, like it's personal now, not business. Claims the family's reputation depends on him winning, like this was some kind of war. Him against Mrs. Dalton. A stupid Desert Storm right here in Mantree."

"People died in Desert Storm, son. Innocent people." Women, children, old men—all because they were in the wrong place at the wrong time.

Gary dropped his gaze to the sand. "Dad says it's the government's fault, letting the environmentalists bully a bunch of politicians into panicking about the ozone layer and dumb stuff like that. He says if the mills can just stay open long enough, all the fuss will get sorted out and the government land will be available for logging again."

"Could be he's right."

"Gramps thinks he is." Gary watched a young hawk circling overhead until it disappeared behind the treetops. The boy had a restless look about him that Murdock understood all too well. Before long the familiar hills and valleys of Mantree would be too confining. And then Gary would itch to try his wings like the hawk.

"What do you think?" he asked when he had Gary's attention again.

"I think this whole thing sucks, that's what!"

This time Murdock's grin was spontaneous and just a touch admiring. "So do I, for what it's worth. But the truth is, neither side much cares what you and I think."

"Tell me about it," Gary muttered. "My dad likes to talk but he's not much at listening. And Grandpa, he just keeps saying it'll all get sorted out sooner or later."

Murdock focused on a spot between the boy's eyes and tried to ignore the queasy feeling in his belly. Whatever was rattling around in his head was giving him fits again, this time affecting his balance.

"Look, Gary, you sound like a sensible kid. And Ardeth seems to like having you around, so I don't have a problem with that. But we need to have an understanding, you and me."

The wariness returned to the boy's eyes. "What about?"

"About visiting hours, for one thing. No hanging around after dark tossing pebbles at her window, no arranging to meet her someplace without her mom or me knowing, things like that. It could be dangerous—for both of you."

Gary flushed, but held his gaze steady. "Nothing's going to happen to her, not while I'm around."

"Glad to hear it." Murdock drew air into his lungs and concentrated on keeping the crashing pain in his head at bay. "And just for the sake of my peace of mind, I'd like your word you'll call before you come visiting."

Defiance crept into his expression again, more from habit, Murdock suspected. "What if I don't? What then?"

"Son, take my word for it, you wouldn't like it." He kept his tone mild, but the flicker of Gary's lashes told him the kid had gotten the message. He gave him a moment to think about it, then extended his hand.

"Do we have a deal?"

Gary's grip was firm, his hand callused and harder than Murdock expected. "Guess we do."

"I'll count on it." He watched long enough to make sure Gary made it to the spot on the other shore, then headed back to his place where he could be sick in private.

Six

The acrid smell of smoke woke him. He was already out of bed and halfway into his jeans when he saw the orange glow through the bedroom window. Some bastard had torched the fields.

Two seconds later, his service weapon snuggled against his spine and his bare feet protected from the brambles by his boots, he was out the door and headed for the river and the irrigation pump. Half the valves were still leaky sieves, waiting for him to replace the old gaskets, but the system was still intact. In any event, it would have to do. It was all they had.

Ordinarily an open field was a risk he wouldn't tackle until he'd reconnoitered the area, but flames were already stabbing the sky. The smoke would have to serve as cover.

He was halfway to the path when he saw B.J. speeding toward him from the direction of the house, her nightshirt flapping against her thighs. She was shouting something about the pump.

"I'll handle it," he shouted without breaking stride. "Go back to the house."

The path was slippery with dew, causing him to skid. His balance failed him, and he went down, but he managed to twist enough to take the impact on one shoulder and roll. He came up staggering, sensing a movement to his left. His pistol was already in his hand as he veered right toward the only cover, a fallen log. Shots came from the tangle of brush near the pump house, a short burst with tracers.

Figuring the distance between him and the shooter at fifty yards, he rolled again, letting go with a burst of his own. From the corner of his eye he saw a flash of white, and then B.J. was crouching next to him behind the log, breathing hard.

"Are you all right?" she demanded, clutching his arm.

"Damn it, don't you *ever* listen?" Furious, he shoved her behind him with the arm she still held, his attention riveted on the brush. Instinct told him the sniper was still there, waiting for him to make a mistake and show himself. Without camouflage, his bare chest would make an optimum target.

As dispassionate as one of Mole's computers, his mind began sorting through his options. He scanned the terrain, looking for the high ground. It was then that his vision started to blur, one image becoming two. Closing one eye might improve his focus, but it would play hell with his aim.

"Can you see who it is?" B.J. whispered close to his ear.

"The guy who set the fire would be my first guess," he answered in a low voice without turning.

"Obviously he doesn't want us to turn on the pump."

"Obviously."

She made a sound that could have been a laugh. "I called the fire department. They should be here soon."

"Don't count on it."

He felt the press of her breasts against his bare back as she leaned closer to whisper, "If you kept him busy, I could—"

"Forget it."

"But—"

"Make one move toward that pump, and I'll deck you."

He heard her swift intake of breath. "You wouldn't dare!"

"I would, and what's more, at the moment, I'd probably enjoy it." That shut her up, but he had a feeling not for long.

"Get down flat," he ordered while he had the advantage. "Put your head down, make like a hole in the ground."

"Listen, this is silly. The guy is probably gone and—"

As if on cue from a bad movie script, the man fired again. Murdock ducked, taking B.J. down with him. He scrambled to cover her, throwing his arms over her head and hunching his shoulders.

Sand flew, and wood splintered as slugs sprayed the area in a ten second burst. Debris spattered his back like buckshot, and he ducked his head tighter until his face was pressed against the back of her neck. Her skin smelled like the bath bubbles she'd always tried to get him to use with her, and every time he took a breath, her hair tickled his nose, but he didn't dare move.

Crushed under Cairn's heavy chest, B.J. squeezed her eyes tight and tried to shut out the noise. Small stones bit into her cheek, and something sharp was pressed against her rib cage. It hurt to breathe. It hurt not to.

Murdock's body was a hard weight against her back, and one thigh was angled over hers, the seam of his jeans rough against her exposed skin.

He was a big man with long bones and layered muscles as springy as steel. Toughened to a lean fitness, he wasn't a man who had much softness to offer a woman, especially when he was using that big hard body as a shield against bullets.

The noise stopped as abruptly as it had started. She lay motionless, too scared to raise her head. Ears ringing and her heart jerking like a jackhammer, she waited for the shooting to start again.

"Don't move," Murdock muttered close to her ear, and she heard the furious snapping of twigs and the pounding of footsteps along the shore.

She was still struggling for breath when she heard the splash of a body hitting the water and the thrash of arms and legs as the man with the gun made his way across the river.

Murdock rolled away from her and twisted to a sitting position. In the glow she saw his eyes. They were wiped clean of emotion, as hard and dangerous as the pistol he still held ready.

If she'd ever doubted his ability to kill before, she didn't doubt it now. Not only could this man kill, she knew now that he *had* killed, and more than once. It wasn't a comforting thought, no matter how she tried to tell herself that under the present circumstances, it might have been necessary.

Half-dazed, she turned over and sat up slowly. The smoke was heavier now, and thick with the green-stick odor of burning canes. Across the river a vehicle roared to life and spun rubber.

"He got away," she muttered, still trying to make her lungs work properly.

Cairn snorted something rude. "If you have to talk, tell me something I don't know."

"Well, excuse me."

She managed a few tentative breaths, then looked around. Her cheek was plastered with wet sand, and her dark eyes had the wide-awake appearance of someone who had just received a shock. Other than that, she looked tousled and ready to blast someone. Satisfied that she was in one piece and not much more than shook up, he got to his feet and jogged to the pump house.

The timer was set for three hours, the pump already holding a prime. He threw the switch and heard the satisfying whine of the engine, followed by the gurgle of water through the intake pipe as the pump began to draw water.

B.J. was on her feet and staring in the direction of the nearest sprinkler head when he emerged from the small shelter and headed her way.

He had time now to give her a more thorough once-over for wounds or signs of shock. He could have saved himself the trouble. She was still pale and shaking badly, but she'd found time to wipe the sand from her face and had bunched her eyebrows in that determined line he'd learned to dread.

By the time he reached her side, water was spewing in a steadily pulsing stream from dozens of rain birds attached to six foot standpipes spaced ten yards apart along four parallel lines. The hiss of water on flame was clearly audible.

"Will that do it, do you think?" she asked when he joined her. Her nightshirt was soaked in patches, her breasts clearly outlined by the thin fabric. Still fueled by adrenaline, his body reacted swiftly, reminding him that even a dying man had needs.

"We'll know soon enough."

They stood for a moment and watched. The hissing grew louder, and smoke billowed upward with even more force. But the glow of the flames seemed dimmer already.

B.J. nursed a small glimmer of hope into a wobbly certainty. Everything would be all right. It *had* to be all right.

"At least there's more pressure since you started replacing the gaskets. When Gar finds out why his stab at arson failed, he'll really be mad at Sam Grady. Or maybe it wasn't Gar at all, but if not, who? I mean, burning a person's field is as despicable as burning his barn—or his house."

She was babbling, but she couldn't seem to think properly. Her knees were none too steady, and she was still having trouble getting enough air into her lungs. Her hands, too, had developed an unfortunate tendency to shake. She'd just had her first taste of real danger, and it had left her feeling far too vulnerable. Neither was a feeling she liked.

"Cairn?" She slanted him a look.

He lifted both eyebrows. "What'd I do wrong this time?"

"Nothing—unless you consider saving my life a mistake."

His cheeks creased into a brief grin. "Let me think about that some before I answer."

She smiled. "Much as it pains me to admit it, you were right all along."

"Well, what do you know. A first." He took no satisfaction in her capitulation. Tonight had proved just how far Tremaine's goons were willing to go. His warning to Sarge might have bought a little time, but not enough. And tonight was only the beginning. Now that they knew he was armed, they wouldn't be so haphazard in their planning.

"Don't look so smug," she muttered. "Everyone has to be right sometime, even you, but don't let it go to your head."

She was the only woman he'd ever known who could be gracious and maddening at the same time. Maybe that was why she'd stuck in his head all these years like a nagging ache, no matter how many other women he tried to put in her place.

"We got lucky tonight, but they'll be back." Only a fool counted on his luck to hold.

"Are you saying there was more than one?" She sounded shocked.

"Had to be, from the extent of the flames in such a short time." He shoved his pistol into the waistband of his jeans. Now that the shooting was over, he was feeling jittery, a man of action without a plan. "My guess would be four men with torches, one at each corner of the field."

Four against the two of them—and three children. B.J. fought off a sudden attack of panic. What if the smell of smoke hadn't awakened her? What if Cairn hadn't been there?

She slanted him a look, struggling to express her gratitude and preserve her pride at the same time. Too busy before to notice much more than the gun in his hand and the coldness in his eyes, she realized that his chest was bare and streaked with the same sand covering her legs, and his stubborn jaw needed the attention of a razor.

She'd seen him in need of a shave before. She'd seen him naked in and out of the shower. She'd even seen him dirty and disheveled after a day of working on that old car he loved. But she'd never seen him quite like this, ready to die for a cause that wasn't even his own. Perhaps even to kill to protect his children.

But wasn't that what a warrior did? Wasn't that exactly the thing she'd condemned him for when they were married?

Stunned at the thought, she stared at his harsh profile, seeing as though for the first time the lonely look of pride around his mouth. Had she really called him a selfish bastard because he'd put his country before his family? Before her and her fears?

Or had she been the selfish one?

She ran her tongue over suddenly dry lips, then froze when she realized he was watching. She pushed her sleep-mussed hair away from her face and managed a wan smile. Her lips felt as numb as the rest of her, as though her body had been fast frozen.

"I'd better get back to the house. The kids will be worried."

"Pull another dumb stunt like this last one," he said slowly and distinctly, "and they'll have reason to worry."

"Protecting my land is not a dumb stunt!" Gratitude was forgotten. He hadn't changed.

"It is when you could end up dead!"

"What about you?" she challenged with as much heat as she could muster. "Those bullets don't have names on them, you know. You could have ended up dead, too."

To her chagrin, tears welled in her eyes, and she turned away before he could see them. She was halfway up the path when she felt pain shoot through the soles of her feet. Crying out, she broke stride but managed to keep going, even though each step was agony.

Murdock saw her stagger and went weak for an instant before he made himself move. She was hobbling badly by the time he reached her.

"It's my feet," she managed to utter through her pain. "I didn't think . . . I just ran. The brambles."

"Why am I not surprised?" he muttered, scooping her into his arms. Her bare arm clung to his shoulder, silky and warm against his naked skin, and her hair tickled his jaw. He jerked his head to the side, muttering something distinctly unworthy of an officer and a gentleman.

"In case you've forgotten, let me remind you, Murdock. No one asked for your help."

"So much for being right," he muttered.

"Oh, shut up!"

Being slung against Murdock's chest like a sack of potatoes was bad enough. Finding herself vividly aware of the distinctly masculine contours of that chest was worse. Discovering that she desperately wanted to snuggle against him and let herself be petted by those big, strong hands was worst of all.

It would pass. It had to pass. Becoming involved with Murdock again was a guaranteed one-way ride to pain. One trip per lifetime was enough. More than enough.

Closing her eyes, she concentrated on other things. The hot bath she would draw as soon as she was alone. The damage to the canes. The calls she would make to the sheriff and her insurance agent. Figuring out a way to get Murdock unstuck from her mind.

"Oh no, the kids are awake," she muttered when they were in sight of the house.

The girls ran to meet them, both in robes and slippers. Without breaking stride, Murdock kept going, aiming for the back door.

"What's wrong?" Ardeth asked, half running, half walking beside him. "We heard a lot of noise that sounded like gunshots. We were going to call the sheriff—"

"Is she hurt?" Emily interrupted. "Should I call 911?"

"I'm fine," B.J. assured them.

"Oh my God, Mom, your feet are all bloody!" Emily's hand went to her mouth, and she looked sick.

"I just stepped on a few thorns, that's all. Really! It doesn't even hurt." Not as bad as her pride, anyway.

When the ragged procession reached the back door, Emily rushed to hold open the screen while Ardeth trailed in Murdock's wake. "Which way to her bedroom?" Murdock asked Ardeth, putting B.J. into even more of a temper.

"I'm not unconscious, you know," she spit out over Ardeth's anxious response. "I can talk sensibly."

"Too bad you can't think sensibly," he muttered, pausing to shift her weight in order to carry her up the narrow staircase. It was a mistake he soon regretted. With each step he took, her breasts rubbed his chest, and her head rested on his shoulder, putting her throat at a perfect angle to receive a man's kiss.

"Mommy?"

Looking up, B.J. spotted Ricky's small face peering through the balusters. "It's okay, sweets. Mommy just stepped on something she shouldn't have."

Somehow he managed to look anxious and curious at the same time. "There's a humongous fire outside. I saw flames and smoke everywhere."

"I know, but the sprinklers are putting it out." At least she prayed they were.

"I wanted to go outside, but Ardie said it was too dangerous."

"Ardie was right."

At the top of the stairs Murdock turned left. "In here," Ardeth said, stepping away from the threshold to the room at the end of the landing.

The bed was bigger than a double, the covers pulled back on one side and the pillow rumpled as though she'd spent a restless night. He deposited her on the wrinkled sheets and stepped back.

She swung her legs over the side and sat up. "I'm fine now. All I want is a bath."

"In a minute. First let's have a look at those scratches."

The children were crowded around, looking scared and anxious. B.J. was just plain mad. That he could handle. Dealing with three worried-sick kids without making things worse was a little trickier.

"Okay, here's the drill. Ardeth, you get the first-aid kit. Em, pour your mother a brandy—"

"We don't have any brandy," B.J. threw in, glaring at him.

"Wine, then. And bring some hot water while you're at it."

"What about me, Cairn?" Ricky piped up anxiously. "What should I do?"

"You help your sister with the water, okay? And don't forget a towel and a washcloth."

They scattered, reminding him of a bunch of untrained but willing recruits on the first day of boot camp.

"You're enjoying this," B.J. accused.

"I can think of a dozen things I'd rather be doing at three a.m., sleep being number one." He was lying. It was damn near impossible being in the same room with B.J. and a bed, and not think about making love to her.

"Then for heavens sake's *go* to bed," she muttered, dropping her gaze to her feet.

Too tired to answer, he squatted on his heels and took first one heel and then the other into his hands. The sand had dried, and the blood had caked, making the scratches stand out against her tan. As gently as he could, he brushed the sand from the wounds, and an unwanted ache tugged at his gut.

He'd seen blood before. Lots of it. He'd even watched some of his own pour through a tube to a buddy while shells whistled overhead and the medics kept their weapons close at hand. He'd just never seen it running down B.J.'s slender ankles before.

His fury returned, along with an overriding frustration that he'd been all but useless out there tonight. "Does that hurt?" he asked without looking up.

"Not much. Just stings a little."

"Some of these scratches are pretty deep. Might even leave scars."

B.J. told herself that it could be any man's big hands running over her skin. A doctor's, for instance. "All the Berrymans had scars. It's part of the life, I guess."

His thumb hit a thorn, and she cried out. His fingers stilled, and his head jerked up. Anger smoldered in his eyes, ready to erupt into something unmanageable. "Sell the damn trees, B.J. Take the money and plant some more."

"I can't, Cairn."

"You mean you won't."

"Okay, won't."

Suddenly it was vitally important to take the strain from his face and the worry from his eyes. For her own peace of mind, she told herself, but an old unwanted concern was tugging at her. Cairn had never been a man to spare himself trouble—or pain. If he was needed, he went, no matter how tired he was or how little rest he'd had between missions.

Once, she'd deluded herself into thinking she could make him so happy at home that he wouldn't want to leave it for the brutal, bloody life he'd lived for so long. She'd been wrong, but that didn't mean she didn't feel an ache inside when she saw how much deeper the lines in his face had etched.

"It's hard to explain, I know. Especially to a man like you who sees everything in black and white, but I couldn't live with myself if I just . . . sold out because someone threatened me or because I got scared all of a sudden." She drew a deep breath, then rushed ahead.

"Over in the Dakotas, the Sioux were offered millions in reparation because the government had taken the Black Hills away from them. The elders met, and said no. The land was more important because it was part of them, their spiritual center. They would settle for nothing less than its rightful return."

She leaned forward, and he caught a whiff of her scent. "My trees are like that for me, Cairn. More than just property that can be bought and sold, part of my soul. I wish you could understand how . . . how deeply I believe that."

Murdock wanted to gather her close and rest her head on his shoulder. He wanted to tell her that he understood, even approved. That he felt that way about the job he'd done for so long, and that when she'd asked him to give it up, it had been as if she had been asking him to amputate the best part of himself. That it had nearly torn him in two because she hadn't understood that about him. Or at least respected it. But what good would it do either of them to resurrect old bitterness?

"There's only one thing I need to understand. You're determined to see this through," he said, standing. "Since I signed on for the duration, I'm as committed as you are."

He reached over to switch on the lamp next to her bed, then went to the window for a look-see. Instead of one sheet of flame, the fire was now scattered, reminding him of bivouac campfires during a training exercise.

"Fire'll be out soon," he said without turning.

"As you said, we lucked out."

"Be a mess to clean up, though."

B.J. winced as his big fist impatiently drew back her mother's handmade chintz-and-lace curtains for a better view. Even though she knew he was probably better educated and certainly better read than she was, he seemed out of place next to delicate lace and cherished heirlooms.

Perhaps it was the pistol tucked into the hollow above his backside that bothered her. Or the way he had of filling any room to bursting, no matter how spacious, just by his presence there. In any event, she was suddenly dry-mouthed and nervous.

"Cairn, I know you're doing this for the girls, but I just want you to know how much I appreciate your help, especially since...well, a lot of men wouldn't lift a finger to help their ex-wives cross the street, let alone put their lives on the line."

Letting the curtains fall into place again, he turned to look at her. "Yeah, I'm a real prince, all right."

His sarcasm puzzled her. "Am I missing something here? I've already admitted that you were right about Cascade and the others, and I'm doing my best to thank you for being, well, a good friend, so how come you have that look on your face again?"

"What look?"

"Like you'd rather be anywhere but here, because if that's true, I understand. Really I do."

"I don't think you do."

"Then tell me. I'm a big girl, I can take it."

He moved toward her so that she had to tilt her head back to keep her eyes level on his. "See that door?"

"Yes, I see it. Why?"

"I've already checked it out. It locks from the inside, if a man were so inclined." His gaze shifted to her throat, and she wondered if he could see the blood surging too fast and too hard beneath the skin.

"You still get to me, B.J., especially here, dressed like that. That's the short version."

B.J. was suddenly far too conscious of the damp fabric over her heart and the tight nipples that were anything but invisible. She thought about pulling up the sheet, then decided that that would be far too obvious—and demeaning to the both of them.

"And the long version?" she asked with a calm she had to fake.

He touched her cheek with the back of his hand, as though testing for fever. "I can't decide if I'm too dumb or too smart to do anything about it."

Her heart was really pounding now, and she was having trouble filling her lungs with enough air to keep her senses from clouding. "Maybe it's not up to you."

His expression turned lazy. She wasn't fooled.

"Maybe we should find out." He drove his fingers into her hair and eased her head backward even farther. A word would stop him. She had only to utter it. She should, but it seemed more important to watch the curve of his mouth.

"Aren't you going to stop me?" he grated.

Her eyes studied him intently, drowsy and dark and just a bit dazed. "I . . . don't think so."

His mouth touched hers in the softest of kisses. Instead of fire inside, she felt the slow uncoiling of tension. It was like silk in a spring breeze, soft and seductive and sweet.

Hands as big and rough as his shouldn't be so soothing against her skin, but they were. Hands that strong shouldn't tremble but they did, and his breathing was far from controlled.

She arched upward, needing his arms around her. He made a sound like a strangled protest, then pulled her closer, only to lift his head abruptly on a muttered curse. An instant later, she heard the scuffle of hurried steps on the stairs.

"Here's the water, Cairn!" Ricky cried as he entered the room, his arms wrapped securely around a large mixing bowl. "I hardly spilled any at all."

"Good for you, honey," B.J. murmured, her smile bright and just the slightest bit wobbly.

For the next twenty minutes or so, while B.J. cuddled Ricky next to her on the pillow, sipped the wine Emily had brought and teased the girls about their long faces, he was busy cleaning and disinfecting the scratches and removing the thorns that were still embedded in her flesh.

Ardeth stood at his elbow, as competent and calm as any battlefield nurse, watching him with eyes disturbingly like his own. It wouldn't be long before she was all grown and on her own.

He'd missed a lot of years with her and Emily. Too many to try to make up in a few short weeks. He'd known that before he made the decision to step back into their lives. He'd accepted the role of an outsider and played it the best way he knew how. When he walked away they might miss having him around for a few days, might even talk about him some over the family dinner table, but then their lives would close in around one another again, and he would be less than a memory.

It was better that way.

It was the only way.

It still hurt like hell.

"Cairn?" He glanced up to find Ardeth staring at him, her expression troubled. "The fire was set, wasn't it?"

"Probably."

"By Gary's dad?" Her eyes pleaded with him to deny it. Because he couldn't, he left it at a shrug. "Whoever it was, he isn't going to be happy to find out the plan failed."

"But the fire . . . the berries. Haven't we lost them?"

"The ones on the outer edges of the fields, yes. But the sprinklers pretty much kept the rest protected."

"Are you sure? I mean, it looked so scary and all."

"Take a look," he said, nodding toward the window. The fire's glow was gone, swallowed by the darkness. The whir-thunk of the sprinklers was muted by the closed windows, but still audible. In another two hours any hot spots that remained would be well doused and harmless.

"And here comes the fire department," Emily muttered over the distant wail of sirens.

"Gee, only an hour late, too." B.J was beginning to feel like a wilted ninny, perched on her messy bed in a still-soggy nightshirt, sipping wine that was going straight to her head while her nut-hard, rough-looking, tough-to-his-bones ex-husband tended to her scratched feet with more care than she gave her most fragile crystal.

The trucks were closer, their sirens insistent. Straightening, Murdock pinned B.J. with a look. "Best take that bath now. I'll handle the fire brigade."

"Be nice, okay? It's probably not their fault they're too late."

"Uh-huh." Murdock jerked a thumb in the direction of the other bedrooms. "One of you help your mom to the bathroom, and the others get on to bed."

Ricky slipped from his mother's hold and climbed from the bed. "Can I come with you to talk to the firemen?" Looking up, he automatically slipped his hand into Murdock's.

"Negative, Rick. You belong in the sack."

The boy looked mystified. "What sack?"

"Cairn means your bed, silly," Ardeth said, scooping him into her arms. "C'mon, I'll tuck you in." She carried him off, still protesting while Emily moved closer to the bed.

"I'll help you to the bathroom, Mom. Just hold on to me, okay?"

Satisfied that his orders were being carried out, Murdock headed for the stairs. Behind him he heard B.J. protesting, and Emily clucking over her like a bossy mother hen. By the time he hit the front door, Ardie was singing Ricky to sleep, and B.J. and Emily were laughing together.

He told himself he wasn't sentimental. That he could walk away without a backward look because he was one tough s.o.b. That he wouldn't miss this place and this family. Most of all he told himself that, damn it, he definitely was not still head-over-heels crazy about the obstinate, adorable woman who was the heart of it all.

Seven

B.J. rested her head on the bath pillow the girls had given her last Christmas and closed her eyes. While she'd been stripping off her ruined nightshirt, Em had filled the old tub with water and bubble bath, put two clean towels on a bench within easy reach, and then dutifully went off to bed, leaving her mother alone.

Some women loved their kitchens, but B.J. favored the bathroom with its ancient fixtures and large window through which she could see her trees mating with the sky.

The tub was big enough for two and deeper than the newer models. The water was a sense junkie's dream, warm and silky and wonderfully soothing against her skin, and the bubbles slipped over her with a delicious slowness whenever she stretched.

Already her worries were fading away, leaving her with a feeling of lightness, and the wine she'd drunk was now a lovely warm glow inside her.

Feeling lazy and pampered and just a teensy bit tipsy, she stretched out a leg and rubbed her big toe against the slick porcelain. The scratches Cairn had tended were still tender, but the water acted as a balm, soothing away much of the sting.

She inhaled slowly, drawing the exotic mix of musk and flowers into her lungs. The bubbles smelled like sex, she thought, a lazy smile drifting over her mouth.

"I thought you might have fallen asleep."

She opened her eyes to find Cairn standing in the doorway. For an instant she thought he was a figment of her drowsy musings. But the grime on his bare chest was real, as were the signs of fatigue on his face.

"What a lovely thought," she murmured, finding it hard to be annoyed by his invasion of her privacy, even though she knew she should be.

He propped a shoulder against the jamb and hooked his thumbs in a couple of empty belt loops. "I came to tell you that the fire's out, the front door's bolted, and I'll lock the back door behind me when I leave."

She blinked through the steam, her tired brain working far too slowly. "Do you think he...they'll be back? Whoever *they* are?"

"I doubt it, but there's always that possibility. If it'll make you sleep easier, I can bunk on the couch downstairs for what's left of the night."

"No, but thanks for the offer." She drew a deep breath, the bubbles covering her breasts moving and shimmering like some kind of soft, slinky material. "I've been trying to figure out what to do next, but I can't seem to get past the urge to smack Garson Tremaine a good one right in that smug-looking grin of his."

Her lips curved into a smile he told himself to ignore, just as he was ignoring the fact that, under the chaste covering of bubbles, she was all bare skin and warm secrets. Straightening, he forced his mind into other channels.

"Can I get you anything before I leave? More wine? Some hot tea?"

"I'm not sure I could summon the energy to drink either one." She regarded him somberly, her lashes drooping again. "Why are you being so nice to me, Cairn?"

"Am I?" He kept his gaze on her face and away from the smooth skin above the waterline where the bubbles were slowly disappearing.

"Mmm. After the way I nagged and complained and dragged my feet for the past week, I wouldn't blame you if you decided to drown me in my own bathtub."

"It's tempting, I admit."

"Go ahead. Right now that just might be a blessing."

His gaze skimmed the length of her, lingering for a half beat on the bright red toes peeping through the froth. Only B.J. would face an arsonist and hot lead barefoot, with polish on her toes. He wanted to shake her. He wanted to make love to her.

"Things'll look better in the morning."

"Better maybe." She opened her eyes and sighed. "Messier, definitely."

"True enough."

The water was beginning to cool, and a slow tinge of embarrassment was beginning to creep through the lethargy. She sank a few inches lower until the bubbles tickled her chin. "We, um, should probably think about a plan."

He should think about getting himself out of her house before the soapy steam softened his brain. "Tomorrow."

She nodded, her eyes drifting out of focus. "I was never shot at before. While it was happening, it didn't seem real." Her gaze shifted, found his. The fear was there now, though she tried to hide it behind a teasing grin. "I can see how you could get hooked on the excitement, bullets whizzing over your head and the adrenaline pumping and all."

Murdock's stomach knotted. Her skin seemed paler in spite of the heat in the small room, and her breathing was ragged. Delayed reaction was like that, rearing up to slam into a person just when everything seemed to be returning to normal. He'd seen seasoned combat veterans turn to green Jell-O in the middle of a rough-and-tumble poker game on the plane returning from a mission—and not because of a busted flush.

He grabbed the nearest towel and knelt by the tub. "Sit up."

"Don't give me orders." She thought she'd put fire into her voice, so why had it come out so faint and shaky? And why were her lips suddenly so dust-dry her tongue couldn't take away the sting?

"Then do as I say. Sit up, and let someone take care of you for a change."

"I'm...fine." She had to force the words out, had to fight to keep her hands from trembling as she lifted them to push him away.

"Yeah, you're fine, all right," he muttered, his jaw tight and his eyes smoldering with what she could only define as rage. Whatever protest she'd been about to make was aborted by the strong arms scooping her from the tub and into warm terry cloth.

He sat on the bench and held her on his lap with one strong arm and rubbed her dry with the other. At the same time he kept up a steady stream of conversation, telling her in no uncertain terms what he thought about the Berryman stubborn streak and what he intended to do to her if she didn't start taking better care of herself.

His expression was dark and fierce and intimidating, but his hand moved in a slow, soothing rhythm, blotting the water and froth from her skin as though she were as easily bruised as the fruit ripening on her vines.

Her eyes filled with tears she refused to shed in front of him—or anyone. "I don't know what you're talking about," she muttered, eyeing the broad shoulder that suddenly looked far too inviting as a place to rest her whirling head. "Besides, the girls are fine, just fine, so I don't know why you're so upset."

He snorted. "I passed upset days ago."

"Then, why—"

"Because damn it, no matter what that piece of paper I signed says, in my head you're still my wife. And I take care of what's mine."

She stared, too shocked to even blink. "But you never...all those years—"

"All those years you were married to someone else."

He tucked the towel around her and then both arms. She was still staring at the clenched-tight thrust of his jaw as he stood and carried her into her bedroom.

His skin was slick from the steam, and his hair was curling over his forehead and clinging like bits of unraveling silk to his neck. She wanted to tell him he needed a haircut. She wanted to tell him he looked worn and tired and far too handsome in a rough-cut, not-quite-civilized way. But the words were locked behind a knotted lump of emotions in her suddenly raw throat.

It wasn't possible to fall in love with the same man twice.

It wasn't smart.

It wasn't convenient. And it definitely wasn't what she'd expected when he'd muscled her into her truck and sped away from the park like some kind of nineteenth-century rogue kidnapping his lady love from the clutches of evil.

It had been melodramatic and embarrassing—and unbearably touching.

Tears welled behind her closed lids and eased through her lashes to run down her cheeks. To her chagrin, she realized she didn't have the strength to wipe them away.

"Don't move. I'm not done with you yet." He deposited her in the nest of pillows she seemed to have left hours and hours earlier, then crossed to the dresser and pulled out drawers one by one until he found the one containing her nightshirts.

He grabbed the one on top, then stifled a groan. It had to be silk, the filmy kind with lace that a man could put his hand right through if he wasn't careful.

Turning, he caught her scrubbing her cheeks with the heel of her hand. His stomach hitched in helpless rage. Imagining Tremaine and his henchmen bloody and behind bars for a lot of years helped damp it down. The rest he managed on will alone.

"I think that wine went to my head more than I thought," she mumbled, meeting his eyes defiantly.

"More likely shock. It's been a hell of a night."

He realized he still clutched her nightgown and held it out. "Not that one," she protested, her voice wobbly. "It's my best one."

He wondered who she was saving it for, managed to bite down on a growl of frustration, and shrugged instead. "Put it on anyway."

She saw the dangerous glint return to his eyes and decided she was too exhausted to stage a major rebellion. Stretching out a hand, she took the nightie from his fingers and then realized she didn't seem to have the strength to do more.

Murdock saw the silk fluttering in her hands as they began to tremble. And her skin was paling again, as though more blood was being sucked from her skin with each ragged breath she took. Tears still slid from eyes that had taken on a stunned glaze, and her lips were white.

He kept the violent curse inside his head, but the need to smash something burned in his veins even as he lifted her into his arms and took her place against the pillows.

"Shh, you'll scare the kids," he murmured, tucking her head against his shoulder and closing his arms around her. A quick glance toward the door reassured him that he'd instinctively kicked it closed behind them. At least he'd done something right, he thought, feeling her shake harder with each muffled sob.

She was trembling, but he could feel the strain in her muscles as she tried to control it. "Let go, honey," he murmured against her hair. "It's better out than in."

"H-how would you know?" she managed between sobs.

"Male intuition." And a lot of practice, only in his case he'd run his pain into the ground, pounding the earth instead of some innocent drunk in a bar someplace, taking out his frustrations on himself where they belonged.

She gave in then, crying hard for several long moments. And then, with a sound like a strangled laugh, she brought herself under control. "It was the sound of the bullets hitting the log, a sort of soft thunk-thunk," she murmured, her head still on his shoulder and her body curled against his under the sheet he'd pulled over both of them. "I keep thinking it could have been flesh and blood." His, she added silently. While she'd been safe tucked beneath his big, vulnerable body. She couldn't quite repress a shudder.

"Nah, the guy had lousy aim."

"Oh yeah, just how do you know that?"

"We're here, aren't we?"

"Thanks to you."

He felt his stomach twist knot-hard. "Don't be so sure about that. I just might have panicked him into shooting in the first place."

His voice had a raw quality that brought her head up so that she could see the deepened creases by his mouth, the added tension around his eyes.

"Hey, you're not feeling guilty by any chance, are you?" she demanded softly.

He moved his shoulders. "It wouldn't be the first time. Probably won't be the last."

Deeply touched to discover just how vulnerable a man can be when he's convinced himself he has to be infallible, she lifted a hand that was steadier now and traced the tense line of his mouth. Her own emotions churned—part gratitude and part guilt. It was her stupidity that had gotten them into this fix in the first place. A large part of her emotions, however, were made up of something that she could only label love.

"Forget the guilt, Murdock," she murmured, knowing that he would shy away from anything that smacked of sentiment. "This time you're not entitled."

His mouth moved beneath her fingertip, relaxing marginally. Because it was Murdock, she counted even that small release of tension a victory.

"Says who?"

"The boss lady, that's who."

His mouth relaxed even more. It wasn't quite a smile, but close. "Never thought I'd end up taking orders from a woman."

"That sounds like the words of an unrepentant chauvinist."

"Guess I still have a lot of Carolina in my blood."

"Guess so." She was proud of the casual smile she mustered. Neither of them could ignore the fact that she was curled against him under the sheet, naked and damp.

Their eyes met. Locked. His eyes lost their tiredness, then slowly heated to a smolder that had her breath catching in her throat. She pulled away, fumbling with the sheet until she was wrapped like a mummy. It didn't help.

Her breathing speeded, became shallow. "I got you all wet."

"Not wet enough. I'm still filthy."

"The water's still in the tub. Be my guest."

His gaze dipped to the swell of her breasts under the swaddling sheet. "Is that what you want?"

His head lifted, and his eyes fixed intently on hers. The message was clear. If he stayed, they would end up making love. The thought had her going hot and cold at the same time.

"I think so, yes."

He nudged her chin higher with his knuckles. "That's not good enough. Yes, or no, I want you to be positive."

She drew a shaky breath. "What about you?"

He crooked one knee, shifting just enough so that her thigh was pressed against his rigid arousal. "Any more questions?"

A laugh bubbled from her, quickly squashed as she pressed her lips together. "Well, that's certainly positive."

His hand closed over her throat, not quite as gentle as it could be. Her skin was warm under his fingertips, her pulse violent and hot, but her eyes showed no fear. Only a deep confusion.

"You're a part of me, B.J.," he said in a voice that was low and dangerous and edged with a barely repressed anger she didn't understand. "I can't cut you away without bleeding to death, but I can't be a permanent part of your life, either."

She had to take a breath before she could answer. Her heart was pounding so hard it was difficult to think. "I . . . know that."

"Know this, too. I want you and I'd kill to keep you and yours safe, but when this is done, I *will* leave. And I won't look back."

He'd said the words because they had to be said, but the slow, deep hurt that came into her eyes nearly had him begging her to forgive him.

As though from a distance, B.J. watched herself smile and marveled at how strong she'd gotten over the years. The cruel words scarcely hurt at all. But then, she'd heard them before, hadn't she? Certainly the meaning, if not the exact words.

"Thank you for being so honest," she murmured, then found her lips painfully dry.

Murdock watched her tongue slide quickly between her pale lips and groaned silently. He couldn't remember being more hungry for a woman. So hungry his control was balanced on a knife's edge, and the pressure in his groin was becoming impossible to ignore. Because all his instincts were screaming at him to make the choice for her, he forced himself to wait.

"I wish you would have just seduced me," she murmured finally.

"I did that once. It didn't work out."

"No," she murmured. "It didn't work out at all."

After a while she'd needed more than great sex. And yet she was tempted. No one had ever made her soar the way Cairn had when he kissed her. No one had left her feeling so fulfilled and feminine and sexy as she drifted off to sleep in his arms. Not even Roger, though she had loved him dearly.

Leaning forward, she pressed her mouth to his. He shuddered, a quick involuntary spasm beyond even his will to contain, and then he was pressing her back against the pillows. "That had better be a yes," he grated, his mouth inches from hers.

"Yes," she murmured, pulling him down to her. "Definitely yes."

His groan was half surrender, half impatience, and delight filled her. His hands were in her hair, his mouth hot on hers, kept gentle, she sensed, by supreme effort.

His size, his superior strength, enthralled the woman in her and made her feel safe. His hard muscles, his long, clever fingers, his musky scent were potent reminders of a barbaric masculinity only partially restrained by the overt trappings of civilization.

Arching upward, she pressed against him, skin separated from skin by only a single frustrating layer of material. The fury of his heartbeat excited her, and the heat of his flesh seared hers.

There was no time for words, no time for wooing. Once released, his passion was irrevocable and demanding. Committed now, she met the probing ferocity of his tongue with an equal ardor that elicited a sound like pain from his taut throat. Quickly, deftly, he stripped the sheet from her, even as he pressed hot kisses along her throat.

Arching back, she invited him to suckle at breasts that were already quivering, to use his lips and tongue on nipples already hard and straining.

He broke contact, but only briefly and only far enough to give his hands and mouth free play over her skin. His commanding hands explored the softness of her breasts, the taut smoothness over her rib cage. With a husband's familiarity, his palm smoothed over the feminine curve of her belly for long, exquisite minutes before trailing lower.

His fingertips burrowed through intimate curls, teasing, tempting, then retreating until she was quivering helplessly. And all the while, his mouth was seducing hers, drawing long, moaning gasps from her throat.

Needing him, loving him, she skimmed her hands over his massive shoulders, slick now with the sweat of desire, and he trembled. Exultant, she dug her fingertips into the thick hair at the nape of his neck, feeling the spring of curl and the ridge of scar tissue that hadn't been there the last time they'd made love.

Later, she would ask about those scars. Now she wanted only to feel. To soar. To burn under the touch of his hands and the throb of his kisses. Impatient, hot inside and out, she arched higher, needy, ready.

But he seemed consumed by the taste of her mouth, even as one hand trailed along the curve of her belly, the delta of her thighs. His arousal prodded her, leaving no question that he wanted her, needed her. Hungered as she hungered.

Her fingers pushed between them until they found the waistband of his jeans. The top button released easily, but the others were pressed tight against her thigh by his weight. Against her. She felt rigid flesh, sexual heat. In his kiss she tasted desperation.

And yet, he waited, as though prolonging his own pleasure as well as hers. Sobbing in frustration, she pushed at him until he eased backward. Nearly frantic now, she tore the buttons free, then pushed at the denim stubbornly keeping him from her. He was naked under the jeans, and she longed to feel the power of his thighs moving against hers, lubricated by the sweat of shared passion.

Freeing one hand, he helped her until there was only rigid passion against a soft nest of coiled black hair. Her hands clutched at him, her moans uncontrolled pleas.

He was breathing hard, his muscles bunched, his face that of a man undergoing torture, and yet he continued to take his time readying her with his hands and mouth.

Helpless, nearly mindless, she writhed and bucked, her hips straining upward, her flesh hot. His kisses were incendiary, igniting a fire in her blood that drove away the last of her restraint. She was a wanton now, poised on the most exquisite edge, wild with her needing. Beyond speech, beyond pleas, she moaned and arched.

As though sensing he could take her no higher, he stilled, resting his hand against the hot mound between her legs. Then slowly, inexorably he slipped his fingers deep, exciting tiny tremors.

Her fingers closed over his wrist, her short nails gouging skin. "You," she pleaded in a tortured whisper. "I want all of you."

His breath hissed through his clenched teeth, and his eyes glittered silver. "I don't want to make you pregnant." His voice was harsh, lashed with effort, and a dull red rode over his strong cheekbones, suggesting a man in deep pain.

She managed a smile, touched to the depths of her soul that he would sacrifice his pleasure to protect her. "Not possible," she managed through lips that were still throbbing from his deep probing kisses. "Surgery...after Ricky."

Shock leaped in his eyes, followed by an expression that might almost be disappointment. She had no time to wonder, however, because in the next instant he was off the bed and tearing at his boots, his jeans.

And then he was pushing her back against the pillows again, his body poised and ready over hers. His arousal was angry, ridged and knotted with power.

With a groan that seemed torn from him, he came down on her, his knees pushing her thighs apart in readiness. He whispered her name, then words she was too far gone to understand, a plea for help. His mouth descended, claimed, branded, and he drove home with no further waiting, no hesitancy, filling her with hot pleasure that rose and rose until she was shuddering and gasping, her fingers opening and closing against his shoulders.

His sensual savagery was exhilarating, his complete lack of control more arousing even than his hands and mouth because it was so rare. Winding her arms around his neck, she matched him thrust for thrust, pleasure for pleasure, her mouth clinging to his as the fire in her built, blazing hotter and hotter until she was consumed by it.

At the moment of release she cried out, a low shuddering gasp of purest fulfillment. As though waiting only for that one unmistakable sign, he thrust once, twice and then gasped out his own release before burying his face in the curve of her neck.

Sheathed inside her, still partially aroused, his body was a part of her. The feeling was sublime, and she closed her eyes, exulting in the radiant bliss filling her.

Languorously, feeling smug, she wrapped her arms around her wild lover's heavily muscled back and hugged him close. "I'm too heavy," he muttered someplace close to her ear.

"Not yet. I'll tell you when."

She thought he chuckled. She felt him relax. "So what else is new?"

His hand was curled around her throat—big, strong, capable of creating pleasure or violence. Like the man himself. Tough, clever, always sure, always steady.

Turning, she pressed a kiss on the back of those long, callused fingers, then closed her eyes and let herself drift. Nothing seemed impossible. No one could hurt her. And, at least for the moment, she was deeply, gloriously in love.

* * *

Murdock woke with his head in the cold, clammy jaws of a vise. He managed to keep from crying out, but the effort nearly gagged him. The room had grown cooler, but his skin was drenched in sweat, and his stomach was queasy.

After months of headaches, he'd learned to gauge the severity of the attacks far too well. This time he wasn't going to get off easy. By the time the pain eased, he would be out cold and grateful for the oblivion.

Next to the bed, the light still burned, and the clock read four-ten. B.J. was sleeping on her side, his hand still clasped in hers. For the first time in his memory, he had allowed himself to be touched while he slept. When had he come to trust her so much? he wondered.

It struck him that he was almost as vulnerable in sleep as he would be in blindness. No matter how acute his other senses, sight was his primary way of relating to the world. His vision was sharper than most, more attuned to subtlety, trained to detect danger. Without it, he would always be open to attack. Worse, he would be an object of pity.

Ignoring the agony in his head, he closed his eyes and tried to imagine what it would be like to live the rest of his days in darkness. Icy panic swept over him even though he knew he could open his eyes and find the room exactly the same. Forcing down the fear, he pressed his fingers against hers, seeing that small hand in his mind.

She had strong fingers and a soothing touch. His mind toyed with the idea of her leading him around, helping him to orient himself to the limitations and restrictions that were to be his forever.

What would it be like to make love to a woman he couldn't see? What would it be like to lie beside her later and listen to the quiet sound of her breathing and know he would never see her face again?

Just the thought of his helplessness had his heart ramming blood at a furious rate, and he was suddenly scared, more scared than he'd ever been in combat. An image of the grotesque tiger cages used by the Vietcong in the war to imprison U.S. POWs came vividly to mind, and he cringed.

That was what blindness would be like, he thought. Holding a man in a cage for all to view his every fumbling move, his every struggle to survive. He thought of B.J. watching those struggles, standing by helplessly because she knew how he would hate her offering to help.

How could a woman possibly love a man who couldn't even protect her from the mildest of threats? How could she bear to have such a man touch her?

The pounding in his head seemed measurably worse, and he drew in a long deep breath, trying to visualize his head filled with warm, golden light the way the Navy therapist had taught him. Anything was better than the drugs he used only as a last resort.

The vise eased its bite, and, because he needed to see her, he risked opening his eyes to the world again. The sheet had slipped to her waist, and she was huddled into a ball against the chill. Gritting his teeth against the pain that invariably came whenever he moved, he slowly pulled the sheet to her shoulders, and at the same time slipped his hand from hers. She frowned in her sleep, her mouth pale and still slightly swollen.

In spite of her doubts and the fear she would consider a weakness, there was a serenity about her that drew him. When she was near, he felt more settled in himself. More grounded to the good and decent things in life instead of the obscene and violent.

Years ago he'd fought hard to resist the order and calm she'd brought to him, knowing instinctively that loving her too much would blunt the killing edge he'd worked so hard to hone in order to stay alive.

Here, with her and the children that would always be his now, no matter where he went, he felt complete. Content. Even, he realized now, happy in ways he'd never expected. Things as simple as an evening meal took on new dimensions when he ate with the family. It was chaos, with two teenagers trading affectionate barbs and a rambunctious little boy machine-gunning questions at him while he and B.J. tried to carry on a rational conversation of their own. A guy had to be crazy to like that kind of noise and confusion. A guy had to be an idiot to give it up.

Moving carefully so as not to wake her, he eased from the bed and straightened to a standing position. The room whirled around him with sickening speed until he willed it still. When he was oriented again, he got into his jeans, shoved his feet into his boots, and then waited for his head to quiet again.

As though sensing she was now alone, B.J. murmured a protest, her lashes fluttering. Still frowning, she rubbed her cheek against the pillow, then sighed and sank into sleep again.

As gently as he could manage, he brushed his knuckles against her cheek, then slowly bent to kiss the top of her head.

I love you, baby, he told her in his mind. Enough to leave when this is over.

And when he did, it would break his heart.

Eight

B.J. poured another cup of coffee, took a quick sip, then turned to face the others still gathered around the breakfast table. Up at six, she'd called Roger's sister in Portland with a quick rundown of the situation and a plea to take in the kids for the duration, fixed a huge country breakfast, then roused her family. She'd even sent Ricky to fetch Cairn from the cabin.

He'd arrived minutes later, freshly shaved and tired-eyed, looking as though he hadn't slept. She'd felt a warm jolt of pleasure all over again, but had managed to keep her morning greeting casual.

"It's all settled. Aunt Margaret is expecting us around noon. Girls, each of you pack enough for a month at least, and, Ardie, I'll need you to help me pack for Ricky. Everyone should be ready to leave by ten."

"Not me," Ardeth said, shaking her head. "I'm staying here."

"Me, too," Emily asserted, looking stubborn.

"Me three," Ricky piped up, then grinned broadly at his own joke.

Cairn said nothing, and his expression telegraphed little. He'd eaten in silence as well, listening and watching with a rock-solid patience she envied. Her own was wearing thin.

B.J. stood a little straighter and, in turn, gave each of her offspring her stern-mother look. "Look, guys, I don't intend to make a big deal out of this, but it's also not up for discussion."

"It's our land, too, isn't it?" Ardeth exchanged a quick look with her sister. "I mean, that's what you've always said."

"Ardie's right, Mom, and we love it, too. So how come you won't let us fight for it the same as you?"

"Because it's dangerous, that's 'how come.'"

"Crossing the street's dangerous," Emily rebutted.

"And driving a car," her sister contributed.

"And don't forget casual sex. That's about as dangerous as you can get these days."

B.J. cleared her throat. "Look, girls, I'm really proud of you for wanting to see this through, but—"

"I wanna stay, too, Mommy! Aren't you proud of me, too?" Ricky sat up straighter, his scrubbed face shining.

"Of course I am, sweets, but I also can't stand the thought of something happening to any one of you, which is why I want you safely out of the county until this is settled."

"Well I'm not going!"

B.J. cast her eyes to the ceiling, hoping for divine wisdom. When none seemed forthcoming, she looked instead toward Cairn. "Maybe you can make them see reason. I don't seem to be having much luck."

A man with sense would take the hint she'd tossed his way and run with it. But then a man with sense wouldn't have gotten himself tangled up with his stubborn ex-wife and her brood of equally stubborn kids in the first place.

"I'm the last person to give advice," he hedged, hoping against hope she'd let it go at that. When she smiled and gestured with one hand, he knew he was sunk.

"No, no, it's okay. Please, go ahead. Tell us what you think."

He cleared his throat and wondered if the yellow streak running up his back was visible to the naked eye. "I think the kids are entitled to choose whether they want to stay or go."

"All *right!*" Out of her chair in a flash, Emily hugged him hard, taking him by surprise. He felt his face burn, and his stomach tighten.

"Way to go, Cairn," Ardie cheered, beaming at him with her mother's incandescent charm.

Was this what it felt like to be a father? he wondered. If it was, he was for it one hundred percent.

"Does that mean we're not going to run away?" Ricky asked, looking confused and excited at the same time.

"It sure does, kiddo," Emily shouted, snatching him off his chair to dance him around the kitchen.

Cairn caught B.J.'s eye and stifled the grin that was already half formed in his mind. Her lips were pressed tightly together and temper seethed in her eyes, primed and ready.

"May I see you outside, please?"

Since she was already halfway to the door, he didn't seem to have much say in the matter. He excused himself and headed for the door, feeling hung over from the painkillers and dull-witted from lack of sleep. Not the best combination to take into what he sensed was going to be a major battle.

She was waiting for him by the pin oak, pacing like a furious lioness about to pounce. It hit him then that B.J. was a magnificent woman. As tough as wire when she had to be and yet, alluring and feminine, even when she was dressed in baggy shorts and a ratty shirt.

He was positive only a select few knew just how feminine.

His body reacted at the memory of the soft curves and secret hollows under that shirt, but it was more than sex he wanted from her. Too bad he'd found that out too late.

"I know, I was out of line, but you asked," he said, hoping to vent some of the steam she'd built. "I figured you wouldn't want me to lie, right?"

"I wanted you to back me up. If that meant lying, then yes, I wanted you to lie!"

That surprised him and he didn't bother to pretend it didn't. "Sorry, I don't lie, not even for you."

Her eyes flashed, more gold than brown in the dappled light, and her mouth went pale. "Bully for you."

Stepping closer, he caught a hint of bath salts and soap, and couldn't help thinking about her warm, soft body nestled in bubbles. It didn't help his mood—or his determination to keep his distance.

"Okay, so I blew it. It happens. So what?"

"So what? So what?" She glanced toward the house, her hands firmly planted on her hips. "I'll tell you what. I'm going to have the devil's own time convincing my kids to leave, now that they know they have you on their side."

He shrugged. "I'm just the hired hand here. You're their mom."

"And you're the girls' father, damn it! Doesn't that mean anything at all to you?"

He'd been hit below the belt before and survived. He'd survive this. It would just take time before the pain stopped being acute enough for him to believe that.

"It takes more than a jolt of semen to be a father. Isn't that the rationale you used when you wanted me to sign away my parental rights to another man?"

B.J. felt the fury drain from her in a sickening rush. Her throat tightened, and she tasted shame. "I didn't mean that the way it sounded, I swear." Shaking now, she went to him but stopped within touching distance, waiting, he presumed, for him to make the first move. Not this time, he thought. He'd pushed hard enough. This time it was up to her to say she was sorry.

"It's just that I . . . that . . ."

Suddenly she couldn't seem to form the right words, and her insides felt queasy. "Oh, Cairn, I'm so scared. What if they had burned the house? What if one of those bullets had hit one of the kids?"

Murdock found it impossible to hang on to his own anger when his tough, determined lady had turned breakable right before his eyes. He wanted to hold her. He wanted to protect her and shield her and pamper her like the fragile woman she suddenly seemed. He told himself she wouldn't want that.

"Forget the 'what ifs,' B.J. They'll only make you crazy, and you can't change the past, no matter how hard you're willing to try."

Her mouth trembled into a small smile. "You sound like you've faced a few 'what ifs' yourself."

"A few." He shifted, uneasy as always when the conversation edged toward personal. "I've learned not to dwell on them."

"Maybe you can teach me your secret. Lord knows, I've been over and over my conversations with Gar Tremaine dozens of times, trying to figure out how I could have headed this off, but if there's an answer, I haven't found it yet."

"Maybe you're asking the wrong questions."

"Maybe."

She snapped a twig from the lowest branch and sniffed the leaves. She lifted her gaze to his, and the full impact of all he'd lost hit hard. "Tell me the truth, Cairn. Am I being pigheaded and naive to think one person can make any kind of difference in this crazy world?"

Cairn dropped his gaze. There was a rock half-buried in the dirt and he kicked it loose with the toe of his boot. Her question wasn't rhetorical, nor, he suspected, asked easily. He had a feeling she was vulnerable enough now to be talked into giving in. To insure her children's absolute safety, if for no other reason.

He wanted them safe as much as she did. He wanted *her* safe. Too bad he knew firsthand what it felt like to ignore emotion in favor of logic. Perhaps, then he could say the words that would make her believe she wouldn't regret the loss of a few trees.

Letting out a long breath, he lifted his head and worked at a smile. "Pigheaded, yeah, but not naive. And yes, I think you can make a difference. I've seen firsthand what one person can do, good and bad. In war it sometimes takes years after the last battle is over to really know who was fighting on the side of the angels. In this case, I'd bet on you." He reached out to tuck a windblown lock of hair behind her ear. "For what it's worth, I'd trust you to cover my back anytime, anywhere."

Her eyes warmed, drawing him. "Is this a battle we can win?"

"No doubt about it."

"I'm still afraid for the children, even though I'm proud of them for wanting to stay."

"They're great kids. You've done a wonderful job with them."

"I had help. Roger was a terrific father, far more patient than I could ever be. And he always had time for them." Her expression turned sad, and her eyes clouded. He felt raw inside. Lonely.

Worse, he felt a grudging respect for the man who'd replaced him.

"They must miss him a lot."

"Not as much as they did. Not since you came into their lives." B.J. felt a prickle of tears behind her eyes. "Ricky wasn't yet three when Roger died. He couldn't understand why his daddy wasn't around anymore."

"Must have been rough on you. Losing Roger, I mean."

"Rough enough. I even took a stab at feeling very, very sorry for myself. I mean, losing one husband was bad enough. But two?" She shook her head.

The wind was picking up, and she caught a definite scent of rain in the air. Better now than next week, when the blueberries would be perfect for picking. And then two weeks later the raspberries. And then—

She drew a ragged breath. "About last night..."

"Having second thoughts already?"

"No, it's not that. I mean, the fire...the adrenaline, I had some wine." She watched a flight of Canada geese overhead and wondered if they'd somehow gotten their seasons mixed. Maybe they were as confused as she was.

"It's not as though we planned it," she added.

"No, we didn't plan it."

"And it's not as though it'll happen again."

"Not if you don't want it to, no."

"It's not that. Oh rats, I don't know what I want. Do you?"

Oh yes, he knew. He wanted the time bomb in his head to go away so that he could stay here and make love to her every night for the rest of their lives.

"What I want right now," he said, smoothing her wind-blown hair, "is to get to work clearing away those burned canes. In case you haven't noticed, this place stinks to high heaven."

That got him the small smile he needed to see. "I've noticed, all right," she said, looking vastly relieved. "As soon as the kids and I get back from town, I'll help."

He frowned. "What's in town?"

"The dentist. It's time for the girls' six month checkup, and Ricky needs new sneakers. We'll have lunch at the Tip Top and be back by two at the latest." Her smile was indulgent. "Just in case you were getting ready to ask."

"I was, and see that you are. Otherwise, I'll come looking for you."

He glanced around, then kissed the tip of her nose. She watched until he disappeared into the equipment shed, then headed for the house.

The phone was ringing when she entered the kitchen. The dirty dishes were still on the table, but all three kids had disappeared. "I'll get it," she shouted, snatching up the receiver.

"Hello?"

"B.J., it's Gar. I just heard about the fire out at your place. I hope no one was hurt."

She thought about the sound of bullets hitting inches from Cairn's back, and wanted to scream obscenities at the man on the other end. But that would be admitting he was getting to her.

"Fortunately, no." She kept her voice cool.

"Ah, that's a relief." She heard him inhale, then blow out smoke. "I called to see if you could use any help cleaning up."

"No, I don't need help, but now that you've offered, I do need something from you, Gar."

"Of course, B.J. Anything at all." His tone was just a touch too hearty, and she bit down on the need to tell him not to gloat just yet.

"I need you to stop this vendetta against me and my children before someone *does* get hurt."

"Now, B.J.—"

"Don't patronize me, Gar, and don't pretend you didn't have something to do with that fire last night, because I know you did. But since no one was hurt, I'm willing to forget about that if you forget about my trees."

"No deal." She heard him take a quick drag. "But I am willing to compromise. Half the trees for half the money."

Nervously she twisted and untwisted the cord around her finger, thinking it through. "You won't clear-cut?"

"Be sensible, B.J. We have to clear-cut, or it's not worth the time and effort. Just bringing in the number of choppers needed would take a big chunk out of our profit margin."

"I thought the idea was to keep the mill open and the men working, not bring in huge profits."

"Certainly, but we have to answer to the board as well, and they're only interested in the bottom line." His voice was still smooth, his tone friendly.

Irritated, she made her own voice sharp and disbelieving. "Have you asked them?"

"No need. I'm the chairman."

"Then I guess we're back where we started. No deal."

There was a short pause. When he spoke again all pretense of friendship was gone from his voice. "That's my final offer, B.J. I'll give you twenty-four hours to change your mind."

Something in his tone had adrenaline flooding her veins and her skin shivering. For the first time she was tempted to give in. But the thought of her magnificent trees turned to wood for condos and the ground left barren and ugly stopped her.

"And then what?" she challenged with contempt in her tone. "Try to burn me out again?"

She didn't like the sound of his answering chuckle. "Let me put it this way, Barbara Jane. Why don't you take a drive to the cemetery and look at the headstone you put on good, old tree-hugging Roger's grave? Seems to me there's room for your name, too."

The line went dead. B.J. slammed down the receiver, then stood with her hand pressed to her belly, shaking.

You arrogant bastard, she thought. I hope you get caught in your own saw blade.

It was past noon by the time they made it to the Tip Top. Usually bustling during the heart of the day, the café was surprisingly empty.

Their waitress, a middle-aged woman named Doris, had been a stranger to B.J. She'd been recently hired, she'd explained in a tired voice, and grateful for the work since her husband had just been laid off at the mill in Myrtle.

"I'm getting tired of the dirty looks we get every time we come into town," Emily muttered, picking at the last soggy french fry on her plate while waiting for Doris to return with dessert. "I feel like I should be wearing a bag on my head."

"Good idea," Ardeth chirped, but her attention was fixed on the front booth where Gary was sitting with three of his buddies. Every so often he would look her way and grin. They'd met three times since that afternoon by the river, always with B.J.'s permission, and always at the farm.

"It's just so unfair." Her second-born rarely gave up on something until she'd dissected it to bare bones. "We're not the only ones who've refused to sell trees on private land, so how come everyone's picking on us?"

B.J. glanced at her watch. They should have skipped dessert. "For the same reason the first settlers to these parts picked on the Indians—greed."

"But the politicians keep saying there has to be a balance, you know, between nature and people, and my last year's history teacher said that the people who didn't fight Hitler and those other dictators were just as much to blame as the soldiers for all the atrocities and things during that war."

B.J. felt a lump settle in her throat. "Which is why I think the people who really count in this town will come to their senses sooner or later and tell Cascade where to get off."

"I hope so," Ardeth muttered. "Gary's still not sure he can sneak away long enough to take me to the fair on Saturday."

"Sweetheart, are you sure this 'intrigue' with Gary is wise? I know you care for each other, but his father's always been pretty hotheaded. If he found out Gary's disobeying him, he could do something rash."

"Gary says he's working on his father. He doesn't like sneaking around any more than I do, but he says his father's the one who's wrong, not us."

Ardeth scraped a nail down the side of her milk glass. B.J. noticed it was newly manicured, and that Ardie was wearing her best shirt and new shorts. She had a feeling her daughter had expected Gary to "accidentally" show up while they were having lunch.

"Be careful, okay? Both of you."

"We will."

The waitress chose that moment to appear with the rest of their order. She'd been friendly earlier. Now she appeared angry about something.

"Thanks, Doris." B.J. offered the waitress a smile, which wasn't returned.

"Don't thank me, lady. The cook just told me who you are, and if'n I didn't need this job so bad, I'd quit before serving you another thing." She stalked off, her fists threatening to bend the heavy tray she was still clutching.

B.J. took another deep breath and picked up her fork. "I guess that means I'd better not ask Doris for a refill on the coffee."

B.J. parked in the shade and handed her purse and parcels to the girls to carry inside for her.

"See that Ricky doesn't get in too much trouble, okay? I'm going to check with Cairn," she said, slamming the door. She hadn't had time to discuss Gar's recent offer with him before leaving for town, and she wanted to get his opinion.

Somewhere in the distant trees, a jay screamed an insult. Overhead, a vapor trail from a lone airliner bisected the nearly cloudless sky, and the river rippled over the rocks where Mudcat Creek emptied its turgid water into the larger, faster stream.

Hearing the distant throb of the tractor, she headed toward the sound. The odor of charred vegetation was still strong. All around she saw scraped earth and streaks of ash and cinder where Cairn had used the tractor's front loader to clear away the evidence of last night's vandalism. Burned canes lay at the far end of the field like a pile of ugly black bones.

Running a quick estimate in her head, she came up with eight or nine acres destroyed in this field alone. The other two were over a small rise and closer to the river.

Through the screen of trees, she spied a glimpse of orange and veered left. The throaty throb of the diesel was louder now. For some reason the familiar sound made her uneasy, and she quickened her steps.

As soon as she topped the gentle slope, she saw the tractor. It was stopped in the middle of a row, the engine still running. The seat was empty.

"Cairn? Where are you?"

Shading her eyes, she turned in a circle, but he didn't seem to be anywhere near. "Cairn?"

Suddenly she remembered Gar's words. Had he sent some more of his henchmen with guns? Had one of them shot Cairn?

Panic stung her throat as she took off running. She found him on the other side of the tractor. He was lying facedown in a tangle of unburned brambles, still as death.

"Oh no, no! *Cairn!*"

Terror ripped through her as she plunged into the waist high canes. Thorns tore at her bare arms and ripped her slacks, but she was oblivious to everything but the large body on the ground.

Bending lower, she eased the brambles away from his head, gasping in horror when she saw the deep scratches on his face and neck.

Frantic, she jerked her T-shirt over her head and used it to wipe away the worst of it, looking for bullet holes. All she found, however, was scratches, as though he'd somehow fallen from the tractor.

But why?

His eyes were closed, his cheek resting on one hand as if he were simply napping. But his skin was gray under the blood, and his breathing was labored.

"Cairn? Can you hear me?"

His eyes opened slowly until they were gray slits. "Be okay...in...a...minute." His hand snagged her wrist and held on. "Pain's all in my head." His mouth quirked, as though he'd made a joke but was too tired to laugh.

"Where? Here?" Frowning, she ran her fingers over his head, feeling for more blood. "These two scratches are pretty deep, just missed your eye, but I don't feel a bump."

"No bump. Just...dizzy."

Keeping his fist wrapped around B.J.'s wrist, he rolled slowly to his back, only to realize too late he'd moved too soon. The pain in his head was still delicately balanced on the edge of unbearable, and the multiple images that reminded him of neon eels wiggling in front of his eyes were making him crazy. The nausea he'd so far managed to fight down threatened worse than ever.

He'd been seasick only once, during a gale on his first midshipman cruise in the North Atlantic. Since then he couldn't imagine ever feeling sicker. Now he realized he'd been dead wrong about that.

When he finally managed to focus, he discovered that she had the worst of the blood mopped from his face and was prodding him into sitting up.

"If I help, do you think you can stand?"

"Don't need help." For some reason he sounded exactly like a man coming off a two day drunk, but he was too busy trying to stand to care.

It took a few minutes and a lot of concentration, but he finally managed to coordinate enough of his muscles to enable him to lurch to his feet.

"Whoa," he muttered, feeling the ground tilt like a crazy carnival ride.

"Hold on to me." Somehow she had his arm draped over her shoulders, coaxing him to use her for a crutch. When he tried to pull away, she swore at him, using words that made him grin in spite of the furiously clanging gong in his head.

She bullied him into putting one foot ahead of the other, then switched to soft encouragement. By concentrating on her voice, he managed to keep the nausea confined to his gut and the worst of the dizziness at bay.

By the time they made it to the hedge of rosebushes, all three kids were swarming around, their voices blending into an angry buzz loud enough to rival the gong.

B.J.'s voice rose over the confusion, sharply commanding but calmer now. "Em, call Dr. Gregory and tell him it's an emergency. Ardie, help me get him in the house—"

"No." Somehow he managed to lift his head and square his shoulders. Sooner or later the attack would pass, and with it, the weakness he hated even more than the paralyzing pain. "My place."

She mumbled something he couldn't catch, but the arm around his waist tightened, urging him to move. The ground was steadier now, his legs stronger, and he was breathing more like a man now instead of a laboring freight train.

By the time she had him inside the cabin and headed for the bedroom, he was able to recognize his surroundings enough to be embarrassed at the mess he'd made of her neat little getaway.

"Looks like the maid didn't show up again." He thought he was damned clever. She didn't. Not if the disgusted snort that greeted his attempt at levity was any indication.

"Ardie, pull back the blanket, yeah, that's it, and the pillow... okay, now you take his other arm."

B.J. felt her knees begin to shake. The man was heavier than he looked, even when he was doing his best to walk without assistance. Stagger was more like it, like the worst drunk she had ever seen. And yet, she knew he hadn't been drinking.

"Help me get him on the bed."

Murdock muttered something about not being an invalid, but he was still pale and his skin was dripping wet.

"Ricky, bring me a towel from the bathroom." The boy spun around, looking as scared as she felt. Later, when this was over, she would take time to soothe his fears and answer every one of the questions already brimming in his eyes.

As soon as Murdock's head eased onto the pillow, he groaned and rolled to his stomach, gripping both sides of the pillow so tightly his knuckles poked white against his skin.

"Mom!" Appearing suddenly in the doorway, Emily clutched the jamb and gasped for breath. "Dr. Gregory's...at the hospital...in...Myrtle." She paused to gulp air, her face beet red. "His nurse said to call the fire department or...take Cairn to Myrtle ourselves."

Murdock never knew for sure what he'd said, but somehow he got B.J. to promise not to do either. And then, like a movie screen fading from vivid color to gray and then black, his awareness blinked out.

Nine

Thirst woke him. His mouth was so dry he couldn't work up a good spit if his life depended on it.

"Here, drink this."

He opened his eyes to discover B.J. bending over him, holding a glass of water close to his mouth with one hand, coaxing his head to lift with the other.

Because he was feeling lousy and frustrated and embarrassed as hell, he said the first thing that occurred to him. It was a particularly foul oath that he immediately regretted.

"Feeling better, are we?" she asked in a voice dripping with saccharine as she moved the glass closer. The glint in her eyes reminded him of a Marine drill instructor he'd had occasion to cross when he'd been a green ensign, so he gave up the idea of preserving what little was left of his pride and drank.

"Easy, not too much at once."

By the time he'd downed the last drop, the pallor had faded from his tanned face, and under a day's growth of beard the muscles had lost the pinched look of pain. B.J. concealed an enormous feeling of relief behind a prim expression.

"The manual does say to always use your seat belt when operating a tractor," she intoned without expression as she set the glass on the nightstand next to the diver's watch she'd removed along with his clothes.

"You know what you can do with that manual, don't you?"

"Tsk, tsk, Murdock. Such language."

His eyes turned dangerous. It didn't take much to realize that keeping him down for another twelve hours as the doctor had strongly recommended was going to be a problem.

"What time is it?"

She glanced at the watch's complicated dial. "Almost six."

This time his oath was more pithy than obscene, and she allowed herself a grin. "I was beginning to think you were going to miss dinner as well as breakfast and lunch."

"I had breakfast."

He sat up slowly, his jaw set. If it hurt, he wasn't going to let it show. As soon as she saw his hand tighten on the sheet, she covered it with hers. His skin was no longer clammy to the touch.

"Maybe you'd better go a little easy. Just in case."

The look he gave her had her backing away toward the closed bedroom door, her hands raised. "Okay, okay, promise to stay where you are for five more minutes and I'll stop fussing."

"I have a better idea," he said, narrowing his gaze. "I'll stay where I am—if you join me."

She jammed her hands in the pockets of her slacks and shook her head. "You need to rest."

Behind her the sun was setting, outlining her body in light. Through the thin fabric of her slacks, he could see the sleek line of her thighs. His body gave a tentative throb, then stirred. Apparently he wasn't as whacked out as he'd figured.

"I've been resting. What I need now is a kiss to wake me up, like in the fairy tales you used to read to Ardie when she was a toddler."

She cocked one eyebrow and gave him a stern look. But she was breathing just a little too fast, and her cheeks were pinker than usual. "Haven't you got that backward? The prince is supposed to kiss Sleeping Beauty."

"That, too."

She folded her arms over her chest and opened negotiations. "One kiss, and then I'll fix you some supper."

"Two, and I'll fix yours."

She was tapping her foot now, deep in thought. He could see that he'd given her a problem, which was only fair, since she'd been a problem for him since the moment he'd seen her again.

"One and a half, and you promise to stay in bed."

"Deal."

He held out his hand, and she took it, allowing him to pull her closer.

"Looks like I owe you a new pair of slacks." His finger traced a dark red swatch high on her thigh, making her shiver. It was part arousal, part reaction to the reminder that it had been his blood soaking through the faded blue cotton.

"Actually, I should have thrown them out months ago. But I was sort of attached to 'em, even though they are disgracefully ratty."

His hand kneaded her thigh, and she felt her breath catch. "Did I ever tell you how unbelievably attracted I am to ratty?"

She shook her head. "And I wouldn't have believed you anyway."

"An officer never lies to his lady." He raised her hand to his mouth and kissed the angry red scratches she'd gotten in her desperate attempt to extricate him from the briers. Instead of pain, she felt a slow, warm pleasure spreading under the skin.

His mouth was warm, his tongue hot as it touched the throb of her pulse on the inside of her wrist. She gasped softly, then stiffened as the fingers of his other hand slipped the button of her waistband free and ran down the zipper.

Expecting serviceable cotton panties, he discovered skimpy silk bordered with lace. When his fingers slid between lace and skin, she drew a sharp breath, then grabbed his wrist.

"Cairn, you promised," she protested in a voice made breathy by the first rush of pleasure. "Just a kiss."

He heard the tension in her voice, saw the glitter in her eyes and the trembling of her lips, and felt himself growing hard under the sheet.

"A kiss and a half," he corrected, his voice raspy with the effort to control his impatience. Leaning forward, he touched his tongue to her sexy little belly button, then stopped breathing when she moaned.

"Don't...do that," she whispered on an indrawn breath as his tongue traced the low-cut outline of her panties. They were French-cut and her worst vice. And she'd been thinking of him when she'd pulled them from the drawer and slipped them over her still-sensitized flesh.

"Those things should be outlawed," he murmured, his breath hot against the vee between her legs. Her hands were in his hair now, tangled in the short, silky strands that looked like a mixture of gold and silver in the light.

His shoulders were hard slabs under bronzed skin, lightly freckled where the sun beat down hardest, and his hands seemed to know exactly where she liked to be kneaded, where she longed to be stroked. Tension flooded her, gathered strength, concentrated low and deep inside her.

Still without kissing her, he pulled her down next to him, his hands busy pushing her T-shirt above her breasts. Paradoxically, her bra was white and plain, designed for comfort. Only a man slowly being driven out of his mind would find it intensely erotic. Only a man who hungered to suckle the hard nipples it contained would consider it unbearably sexy.

"Damn hook's stuck," he muttered, his fingers suddenly turned to thumbs. The noise she made was half triumphant, half impatient as she pushed his hands away and freed it herself.

Released from confinement, her breasts were swollen, the nipples aching for the feel of his mouth and tongue. Beyond reason, she helped him rid her of her shirt and bra. His fingers were sure now and patient, leaving her shaking and helpless and struggling to remember why she had to stop him.

"Wait!" She worked to gather the thoughts he was busy scattering. "I...we can't...shouldn't..."

"Shh, we can and we are." His voice was low, seductive. Commanding.

He laid her flat, then cupped one of her breasts in his hand and lowered his mouth. It was as provocative as the first time.

Better.

Her head was spinning and she was nearly giddy with pleasure. Sensation and emotion were blended, inseparable, and all centered on him and the way he was making her feel.

She was willing to go where he led, her trust complete, her love for him as potent as his touch. Later she would think. Later she would rebuild walls. Later she would mourn for what could never be.

Now she wanted his heat and his strength and his courage. Now she needed, hungered, wanting to ride the wild streak in him as far and as high as he could take her.

Shuddering without realizing it, moaning without restraint, she writhed and twisted, as pliant as warm wax. His to mold. His alone.

And yet, even as she relinquished herself heart and soul to him, the need in her to possess as she was being possessed was rising. Her hands were as eager as his now, her mouth hot on his neck, her tongue lapping the salty heat of his skin.

He groaned, going down for the third time, drowning in need. His world had come down to this bed, this woman, and the light she brought to the black hole in his soul.

It was almost a relief to admit to himself just how vulnerable he was to her, how utterly defenseless. If God was merciful, her image would be the last he had before he died.

"Kiss me," she whispered, her body molded to his.

"Thought you'd never ask." His mouth took hers with a drowning man's fierceness. All the years he'd spent missing her narrowed to minutes. All the words he'd wasted convincing himself he had made the right choice twelve years ago seemed hollow.

Now she was the one setting the rhythm, her helpless moans his guide. Her hands pushed and he rolled, his mouth still welded to hers. And then she was taking him places he'd never been before, using her hands, her mouth, words he barely heard over the thundering of his heart and helpless rasp of his breathing.

She was his life, his reason, his sanity. Everything he valued, everything he revered and cherished was wrapped up in her. Even a strong man would break, and she had broken him.

Now he was the one shuddering, the one calling out her name over and over as she mounted him, taking him into the warm protection of her body slowly, letting herself be guided by his desperate groans.

When he was buried inside her, she began to move, her thighs like hot honey against his flesh. He couldn't reason. He couldn't breathe. Inside he burned. He moaned helplessly as wave after wave tumbled him wildly.

B.J. froze, his cries finally penetrating the sensual haze gripping her. He sounded as though he were suffering terribly.

Fighting to clear her head, she searched his face, seeing the taut stretch of muscle along his jaw and the lines of intense strain radiating from his closed eyes.

Guilt slammed into her with locomotive strength, and she cursed through clenched teeth.

It took him a moment to realize that something was wrong. Through a mist of wild pleasure, he saw the stricken look on her face. Her eyes were midnight dark and laced with a terrible worry.

"What?" he managed to push out through the sensations still pulsing in him.

"Are you all right?" She sounded frantic.

"Better than that, thanks to you." It was a new experience for him, being on the downward slope of a sexual high and not being the one in control. "How 'bout you?"

"Fine." Her voice had a definite quaver, and her mouth, besides looking irresistibly enticing, was tense.

"You don't sound fine." He ran his palms up her arms and felt tension under the warm flesh. "But maybe we can do something about that."

He tightened his grip, intending to draw her to him, but she surprised him by going totally stiff. "No, Cairn. We've already taken too many chances."

"Chances? But you said you couldn't get pregnant."

She drew a swift breath, making her bare breasts sway. "Not with me, with you."

"Me? What the hell are you talking about?"

"Your head. We shouldn't..."

"Hey, I won't break," he said, still coming down from the hot, hard ride she'd just taken him on. "And my head's fine. Harder than most, or so you told me once, remember?"

Instead of answering, she slowly eased free, as though she were afraid of making a sudden move. He sensed her panic now, as though she were spooked and ready to run.

"B.J., look at me."

She didn't want to, but she did, briefly. And then she was scrambling off the bed and throwing on her clothes. "I, um, have to check on the kids."

"What I'd do to tick you off this time?"

She flicked him a quick frown that was more distracted than angry. "Nothing. It's just late, that's all."

She was slipping her feet into her shoes by the time he got off the bed, stark naked and still half-aroused. Glancing up, she gasped. "What are you doing out of bed? You need rest."

"Wrong. I need some straight answers." He caught her by the arms, immobilizing her before she could flee.

"Please, Cairn. Captain Frundt said you shouldn't have any strenuous exertion for at least twenty-four hours." And no stress, physical or emotional. Particularly physical.

He went completely still. Only his eyes seemed alive as they bored into her. "Sounds like you were one busy lady while I was asleep."

"Not as busy as you might think, actually. Captain Frundt just happened to be in his office when I called. And when I mentioned your name, he didn't waste a lot of time, especially when I told him what happened."

Her sudden calm seemed to throw him, and she counted that as a victory, however small.

"As a matter of curiosity, how did you know to call Frundt?" He sounded bored. She wasn't fooled. When his drawl turned lazier than usual and his mouth slanted up on the left side, he was ready to strike.

"From the pills in the bathroom. When I couldn't reach Joe Gregory to find out if it would be safe to give you a couple, I called Bethesda. Captain Frundt's name was on the bottle. He said for you to give him a call."

He released her and turned away. "I intend to."

The icy threat in his tone alarmed her and she went to him. He allowed her fingers to remain on his arm for a beat before shaking her off.

"Cairn, he was just trying to help."

He ripped open the top drawer of the cheap pine dresser and pulled out a pair of briefs. "How? By scaring you half to death?"

He pulled on his briefs with quick, sure movements, and B.J. wondered for an instant if she'd only imagined the pain that had all but paralysed him less than four hours earlier.

"No, of course not."

He hauled on socks, clean jeans, a shirt pulled at random from the closet, then turned to look at her. For an instant she thought she saw anguish in his eyes, and then it was gone.

"Don't worry, B.J. It's the shrapnel in my head that's going to kill me, not making love."

"K-kill you? You mean you're dying?" Her voice was shaking, her lips white. Murdock took one look at the horror dawning in her eyes and realized he'd blown it. "But Frundt said you'd had a head injury, that you were still recovering. That's why he thought you should stay in b-bed." The last of the color drained from her face.

She groped behind her for the bed, lowering herself slowly to the mattress. Murdock went to her and would have taken her into his arms, but the sudden panic in her eyes stopped him cold. "No! Don't touch me. I'll...be okay if you don't touch me."

She took a deep breath, desperate to maintain control. She knew she would shatter if that control cracked even a little. "Tell me the rest. All of it, please."

Murdock shoved his hands in his pockets and looked down at her. She was trying so hard to remain calm, but the faint trembling of her lips gave her away. Seeing that small movement she couldn't quite control for all her trying had him wanting to pound walls and break things.

"I took some shrapnel, here." He touched the back of his head where she'd felt the scars the night before. "It's still in there, close to some important nerves. Sooner or later, it will shift."

She held her head very still and her eyes fixed on his. They were glazed with shock and shiny with tears. "And then you'll be dead?"

"Yes, then I'll be dead."

"I . . . see." She sat very still, her hands folded primly in her lap, her back straight. Like a good little girl in church. "Thank you for telling me the truth, although I wish you'd told me sooner."

"Why?"

She dug deep for a smile. It felt shaky on the inside, but it seemed to work on her face. "Because then maybe, just maybe, I might not have fallen in love with you again."

For a minute Murdock thought he was going to be sick. This time it wasn't his head that hurt, but his soul, and the pain was excruciating.

"I'm sorry," he said, his voice raw. "I never meant for that to happen."

"Of course you didn't." Her voice was very soft. He wished she would have screamed at him instead. Maybe then he wouldn't feel so destroyed inside.

"I should have told you, but I didn't want you to worry."

"How very considerate. Thank you."

Keeping him at bay with a look, she got to her feet, swaying only slightly. Cairn held out his hand to her, only to have her shake her head. "I'll be fine, really, I will. Right now, though, I need to be alone."

Murdock sensed that she was hanging on to her control by the thinnest thread. He understood her need for solitude, but he was desperately afraid to let her go.

"I'll walk you to the house."

"No." Her tone was barely audible. "The children will worry."

Like the gentleman his mama had raised, he walked to the door and opened it politely. Still she didn't move, and he realized she was waiting until he stepped back, out of her way.

Without looking at him, she straightened her slim shoulders and walked with careful steps past him and out of the room.

Rigidly at attention, Murdock closed his eyes and listened blindly to the sound of her footsteps echoing on the bare floor. It was only when the outer door closed behind her that he opened them again.

The room blurred, worse than it ever had before. This time, however, his head wasn't the cause.

The children had been in bed for hours, and the house had that settled feeling. B.J. was standing by her bedroom window, looking out. It was a beautiful night. A night for magic.

The sky was clear, a deep midnight blue shading to purple velvet. The stars were out in profusion, and a ripe moon was rising over the trees. Through the open window B.J. heard the chirp of crickets and the slippery slide of the river over the rocks.

The air was still faintly scented with smoke, but was more pleasant now, and the leaves outside her window rustled seductively.

Next to her bed she'd placed a single candle, pure white and scented with rose oil. The only light in the room, its flickering flame cast graceful shadows on the wall.

She heard Cairn's step on the stairs a few seconds before he appeared in the doorway. "I knew you'd come," she said, turning to face him.

Silhouetted against the soft glow of the hall night-light, his body seemed strong and fit, with a swimmer's deep, powerful chest and long, heavily muscled legs. Dressed in jeans and a blue work shirt, he seemed very much a part of the life she'd made in this place.

"Are you all right?" His voice was deep, and she knew he'd been worrying about her.

"Yes. I've done my crying, and I've done my praying." She walked toward him, her gown billowing behind her in a cloud of pale blue silk. She drew him into the room and closed the door behind him. With her eyes still fastened on his, she turned the key in the lock, then smiled up at him, her hands skimming his corded arms.

"Please make love to me tonight, Cairn."

His eyes roamed her face, beautifully dark with love in the candlelight. It was only an illusion, she knew, but tonight was a night of illusion.

"I'm not sure I can."

"Your head?" she asked quickly, her resolve faltering.

His mouth took on a slant she didn't recognize. "No, sweetheart, another part of my anatomy. You darn near wore me out this afternoon."

"Did I? Hmm, interesting." She cocked her head and studied his face. "You don't look worn out."

"I don't?" His body was still rigid, but a smile was waiting in his eyes. She was determined to have it for her own, perhaps the last she would ever have.

"In fact, you look very sexy." Her fingers slipped the top button of his shirt free and then the next. When her fingertips skimmed over his skin, he couldn't quite keep his reaction hidden. Eyes glowing, she slowly tugged the shirt from his jeans, loving the sibilant noise of fabric sliding against his hard belly.

"Are you flirting with me, Miss Berryman?"

"Of course not, sir. Oregon girls don't know how to flirt, but just for you, I could learn."

She slipped another button free, then ran her fingernail along the edge of his opened shirt. He breathed in hard, then grasped her wrists. She loved the callused strength of his hands and the hint of possessiveness in his touch.

"This Oregon girl seems to be doing just fine."

Conscious that his breathing had altered, she tugged her hands free and smoothed her palms over his chest to rest on his shoulders. At the same time she arched upward until her lips found the vulnerable area below his ear.

"Are you sure I don't need a few . . . lessons?"

He sucked in air. "Not if I value my sanity, you don't."

Her heart tumbled at the throaty rasp in his tone. No matter what happened later, tonight he was hers. She prayed she wouldn't lose her nerve.

His arms came around her, holding her loosely, as though he were afraid to crush her small bones. Dropping his head, he nuzzled the perfumed skin of her throat.

"You smell like roses." His voice dipped low, thickened with pleasure.

"You smell like shaving soap," she murmured, touching the hard plane of his cheek. "Such a sexy scent, shaving soap."

He chuckled, a commonplace sound for others, but not for someone existing under a sentence of death. "Damned if I wasn't thinking the same about roses."

His fingers slipped the thin strap of her gown free of her shoulders, baring more of her skin for his mouth to sample. This time she was the one trembling.

Now he turned his attention to the other shoulder, freeing the strap with maddening slowness. His mouth skimmed the slope of her shoulder, ultimately finding the scented hollow of her throat.

Her breath grew shorter, catching in her chest when his tongue gently touched the beating pulse below the skin. "My beautiful wife," he murmured, his rich deep voice so very gentle. "I need you tonight,"

"As I need you," she whispered, her heart racing.

Inching backward until he could see her face, he allowed himself to bathe in the love shining in her eyes. She was his only love, his hope, the light in his soul.

His fingers trembled as they moved the gown away from her breasts. With a sound like a sigh, the wisp of silk drifted to the floor. Reverently, his heart in his throat, he bent to kiss each dark nipple in turn.

He was breathing hard now, but he resisted the need to suckle greedily. Instead, he used his teeth and his tongue, teasing each nipple into rigid pebbles. With each swath of his tongue, her fingers dug deeper into his shoulders and her head arched back on a low moan.

With a groan of his own, he urged her backward toward the bed that was waiting, the covers neatly folded back, the pillows plump and inviting.

Standing by the bed, she freed the last of his shirt buttons, then slipped the fabric free of his shoulders, her fingertips silky on his skin. He would remember her touch always, no matter where he might be, and in remembering, he would love her in his mind one more time.

"I want you naked," she whispered, shaken a little by her own boldness, but utterly truthful. Tonight was a time of truth.

His hands went to his belt, but she pushed them away. "Let me."

Her hands freed the metal button, ran down the zipper, urged the low-riding jeans from his hips. His thoughts scattered, then reformed as he shed his moccasins and rid himself of his jeans.

Standing again, he shivered when her fingers slipped beneath the elastic of his briefs, his need evident in the rigid bulge behind the fly.

Impatient, he finished the task she'd started, shucking off the skivvies with a hand that was shaking. His need was acute, pressuring him to swiftly take what she offered, relieving the growing ache in his groin. But he made himself wait.

Tonight he wanted to make love to her as never before, exposing the most deeply buried longings of his heart for the first and last time.

Gently, he took her to the mattress, his gaze never leaving the exquisite loveliness of her face. The candlelight brought out every nuance of her beauty, touching him in ways that humbled him.

Releasing the last of his self-imposed restraint, he whispered words of love and longing. Reverent words. Words of praise for her beauty and her spirit.

B.J. was consumed by pleasure, driven by the pressure building low inside her. His hands stroked and petted, his mouth worshipped and coaxed, and she could feel the sheet beneath her, the heat of his skin, the thud of his heart. Her veins seemed filled with the most intoxicating of vintage wines, her skin fluid and warm. Nothing had ever been more wonderful, more perfect.

"Easy, sweetheart," he murmured as she writhed beneath his touch, his kiss. "Let me show you what I've never been able to say."

Moaning, she gave herself to him. It was sublime, a feast of sensations, a sublime symphony created by a master. When at last she could take no more, he straddled her, easing into her slowly, watching passion bloom in her face. Candlelight played over her closed lids, making shadows of her long lashes.

His skin, slick with his own raging passion, moved against hers, drawing moans from her, from him. And still he waited, needing to see the play of emotion on her face, needing desperately to feel her warmth enfold him.

When she whimpered and reached for him, he gentled her with a kiss. When she sobbed his name, he thrust slowly, then eased back, his own need close to unbearable.

And then he probed deeper, feeling her moans ripple through her body. She was tossing her head side to side now, whispering his name over and over.

Pleasure came suddenly, hot and sharp and then soaring. She was awash, carried on a crescendo of ecstasy. Her arms were around him, holding him close.

He fought for breath, knowing that she was utterly his, knowing that he was hers. He thrust deep, feeling the swift sharp bite of pain before the pleasure took him higher and higher.

On a muffled sob, she held him tighter, wrapping her legs around him, possessing him. Loving him.

She was smiling in her sleep. The candle had burned low, but the flame was still alive, bathing her face in a soft glow. He had slept briefly, then awakened to watch her.

It wouldn't be long before he had to leave. Tension was running high in the valley, ready to explode. His instincts said that would happen soon.

There was a calm in him now that hadn't been there before. A kind of peace that admitting his love for B.J. had brought him. It seemed so clear now, how desperate his need for that love had become. How desperate it had always been.

The trouble in his soul hadn't been self-doubt or a need for more discipline or a thirst for danger. It had been a lack, an emptiness. In spite of the things he'd done and the places he'd been, he was a lonely, lonely man, living a sterile life. Even if he wanted to change, and he was almost sure he did, he had run out of chances.

Knowing that was like having a knife twisting in his belly. A knife he himself had honed. The irony should have been funny. Maybe it was. At the moment he didn't feel like laughing.

He watched the candle's flame and tried to figure out what he did feel. Regret, certainly. Rage and frustration were a given. And a sadness that seemed to come from a place inside he hadn't even known existed until this moment.

His fingers weren't quite steady as they toyed with the soft tangle of brown hair spread on the pillow. His need to protect her and her children was nearly as fierce as his love.

He'd been just plain dumb to think he could spend time with his girls and not fall in love with them all over again. And Ricky, now there was a kid any man would be proud to call his son.

He drew a long breath, feeling the heaviness settle in his chest again. He would miss them all when he left. And he would always wonder what it would have been like to openly acknowledge those kids as his. To have them introduce him as their father. His heart hurt at the memory of the baby she'd lost.

A little boy.

As though sensing his thoughts, B.J. suddenly sighed in her sleep, and her smile disappeared. Tiny lines formed between her silky eyebrows as though her dreams were suddenly troubling.

A longing to stay came over him, so strong it stopped his breath. He could find a reason. An excuse. And then what? Leave her grieving for another dead husband? No, that he would not do.

He'd been lucky once, when the fall from the tractor hadn't killed him. He wasn't foolish enough to press his luck much farther than that.

His gaze rested on the curve of his wife's mouth. One last taste was all he would allow himself, and then he had to leave her bed. Dawn was breaking, and he had things to do.

B.J. heard the door close with a soft click and released the breath she'd been holding.

She'd been dreaming that he'd already left when she'd felt his kiss. Gentle as a whisper in the dark, his mouth had touched hers. And then he was easing from her bed.

Keeping her eyes closed, she'd heard the rustle of his clothes as he'd slipped into them. She'd wanted to weep when he'd blown out the candle before moving silent as a shadow to the door.

It had taken all of her control to keep from calling out to him, but it was better this way. The night was over, and she hadn't dissolved into tears or pleaded with him to stay.

But, dear God, how she wanted to do both.

Tears filled her eyes, the same tears she'd promised him he'd never see again, and her throat ached from the effort she'd made to keep silent. Burying her face in the pillow he'd shared, she let them come, her muffled sobs shaking her to the bone.

She couldn't bear to lose him again.

But she would, and this time, it would be forever.

Ten

Hayden Tremaine flicked the rod with perfect precision and let out line. The fly landed within an inch of his target, and he let it drift with the current for a foot or so before reeling it in.

"Mr. Tremaine?"

Turning, he saw a man standing on the shore next to his tackle and creel. A logger, from the hard-bitten look of him, and a good one, if the breadth of shoulder and depth of his big chest were accurate measures.

"'Morning, son. Beautiful day for fishing, isn't it?"

"Used to be, in Carolina where I grew up, anyway."

Hayden was intrigued. They got their share of southern transplants in the Northwest, but the man's speech sounded more cultured than cracker. "Something I can do for you, sir?" he asked, watching the man's face.

"Yes, sir. You can tell your son to stop the war against B.J. Dalton before someone gets killed."

Hayden knew then who this man had to be. B.J.'s new hired hand, the one who'd decked Sarge Crookshank with one punch. His curiosity kindled, but he was too experienced at bargaining to let it show.

"War seems like a pretty strong word to use for a business deal."

Hayden shouldered his rod and waded toward shore. The other man watched silently, seemingly relaxed. He wasn't fooled.

Closer now, he saw the shotgun in the crook of his visitor's elbow. It was hinged open, showing empty barrels, a sign in frontier days of peaceful intent. That he'd brought the gun at all, however, signaled a willingness to use it if necessary.

Stepping onto the bank, Hayden felt his blood chill. His son was in more trouble than he knew.

"I've been told you're an honorable man, Mr. Tremaine. Tough, but fair. I never figured you for a coward."

Tremaine's face burned. Buying time to let his temper cool, he bent to place his rod and reel on the soft grass. "Care to explain that?" he asked when he'd had straightened again.

"Where I'm from, a man who had differences with another man—or woman—settles it in private, and he settles it fair. Arson is the weapon of a sneak—and a coward."

Tremaine held the man's gaze. "I agree," he said quietly. "And I hope you believe me when I say I had nothing to do with that fire."

Murdock studied the man's face, looking for deceit. Instead he saw the calm, proud eyes of a self-made man, shrewd, to be sure, and self-assured, but not cowardly.

"I believe you," he said. "But we still have us a problem here."

"How so?"

Murdock shifted his feet, then glanced toward the west. The farm was over the next ridge, and on it, his family, everything he valued in life. He'd been away from them longer than he'd planned. But finding the right shotgun had taken time. Tracking down the elder Tremaine had taken more.

"I don't have a lot of time to waste, Mr. Tremaine. Before I leave here, I need to know that B.J. and her children are safe. If I have to kill your son to ensure that, I will."

Hayden let the shock settle and his suddenly racing heart slow before he nodded. "I believe you would do just that, son. And I believe you know just how to do that without raising a ruckus. Or am I wrong about that?"

Murdock realized he'd underestimated the old man. He was not only shrewd but tough as an old hickory burl. In another lifetime they might have been friends.

"You're not wrong."

Hayden allowed himself a deep breath. The air smelled woodsy, with just a touch of ripe river grunge thrown in. "In that case, one of us had better give that same message to my son. I'd prefer it to be me."

"Today?"

"Today."

Murdock nodded. "Agreed."

He turned to leave, but stopped when Hayden called out. "One more thing, Mr. . . ."

"Murdock. Cairn Murdock."

The old man cocked one sparse eyebrow, a cagey look on his face. He'd served in World War I. Men like this one had come home with a chest full of ribbons—if they'd come home at all. "Colonel Murdock?"

"Commander, retired."

"Voluntarily?"

"No."

Hayden nodded. "One more thing, Commander. You said you didn't have much time. Just when do you plan to leave."

"As soon as you give me your word I won't have to come back looking for your son. Or you."

"You'll have it by midnight—or not at all."

"Then I'll leave tomorrow." The two exchanged a long look of total understanding before Murdock nodded once, turned on his heel and left.

It took some doing, but Murdock finally got B.J., both girls and, because Ricky went where he went, the boy behind the shed.

He'd all but dragged Emily down from the attic where she'd been sorting old photos for an album she planned to make, looking oddly distracted and nervous all of a sudden when he'd appeared, as though he'd caught her doing something shameful.

Ardeth had been in the bathroom, twisting funny looking rods around hanks of hair until she looked like a victim of electrical shock. B.J., on the other hand, looked adorably mussed from a hated bout with paperwork. For some reason he could never understand, she always twisted her hair into little spirals while she worked with figures.

"Okay, you wanted us all together, we're all together," she muttered, her grin saucy. "What next?"

"Let me ask you something first. Does anyone know how to use a gun?"

Surprised, the girls looked at each other, and then at their mother, who shook her head. "Roger didn't believe in guns."

Too bad the kids who shot him did, he thought. "What about you? Do you believe in them?"

B.J. took a deep breath, then let it out slowly. "Let's say I'm just glad you're a better shot than the guy by the pump house."

Satisfied, Murdock reached into his boot for his automatic.

"Wow, a real gun!" Ricky said with obvious reverence. "Can I hold it?"

Cairn glanced at B.J. He expected her to object. Instead, she smiled crookedly and nodded. "If you think it's okay, so do I."

Murdock ejected the clip, checked to make sure the chamber was empty and handed over the gun, grip first. Ricky's eyes were bright, his expression awestruck. "It's a lot heavier than my water pistol."

"A lot deadlier, too."

He let the boy hold the weapon a moment longer, then took it from him and reloaded. "There's no time to teach you how to use this one, so I think a shotgun would be the best bet. One with a light pull and not too heavy to lift, like a coach gun."

"What kind of gun is that?" Ricky asked eagerly.

"The kind they used to carry on stagecoaches to protect the gold," Murdock told him with a grin. "Hence the expression, riding shotgun."

"Oh yeah," Emily muttered. "Now I get it."

After returning his automatic to his boot, he retrieved the twelve-gauge Stoeger from inside the shed where he'd hidden it earlier.

"Gary would love that," Ardeth exclaimed, looking interested.

"Not if it was pointed his way," Emily said with an irreverent grin.

"Shut up," her sister groused.

"Make me."

"Girls, please," B.J. put in, her patience ebbing. "Let's just get on with the lesson." She shifted her gaze to Cairn's face and smiled wryly. "I assume that's why you rounded us all up."

"Smart lady."

"Hear that, kids?" she teased, fighting to keep her chin up and her hands from shaking. Had it only been a day and a night since she'd found out his secret? It seemed a lifetime. So far she'd kept the vow she'd made to herself to keep her grieving private.

Murdock released the lever and cracked the gun open over his forearm. From the pocket of his jeans he took two shells. "These are blanks, but the ones you'll really use have what's called a light load. That means it'll get the job done, if you're not too far from your target."

B.J. winced. "You mean . . . kill someone?"

"Probably not, but a load like this will stop a man my size or bigger from killing you."

Ricky looked impressed. The girls seemed more wary. Murdock smiled at each in turn. "Who goes first?"

They exchanged looks, then Emily stepped forward. "Who's afraid of a big bad gun anyway?" she declared, throwing back her shoulders.

While everyone watched, Murdock showed her how to load the shells into the chamber and snap the gun closed and get ready to shoot.

"Hold the gun under your arm. No, not against your shoulder, under your arm. Like you're carrying a package." Without fuss, Emily did as she was told, then waited for further instructions.

"Pretend there's a man coming toward you. He's going to kill you, no question. Don't think, just react. Aim for the chest, and pull the triggers. One at a time, though, or you'll end up on the ground. This baby has a kick."

"Pull the trigger, huh?" Emily swallowed hard. "What if I do something wrong?"

"Don't worry. There's no shot in these shells. They're designed for practice."

"You're the expert."

With a jerk and a roar, the gun went off, surprising everyone but him. B.J. cried out. Ricky covered his ears. Ardeth giggled, and Emily looked dumbfounded.

"I guess I missed," she muttered, staring at the barrels, which were pointed straight down.

"If those shells had been real, you would have shot off your own foot," Ardeth offered helpfully.

"Okay, smarty, if you think it's so easy, you try it." Emily shoved the gun toward her sister, who suddenly looked a bit queasy.

Muttering to herself, she took the shell Murdock handed her, chambered it awkwardly but successfully, then snapped the gun closed, she took aim at an imaginary enemy.

"Squeeze the trigger, don't jerk," Murdock suggested in a calm tone. "And expect a recoil."

Ardeth spared him a long-suffering look, then nodded. Bracing herself, she took a deep breath and squeezed. Powder exploded, and the gun jerked, but the barrel stayed up.

"That would have been a successful shot," Murdock praised, taking the gun from her. "You just saved your own life and maybe mine."

Ardeth giggled. "Just call me Annie Oakley."

"Oh Lord," Emily muttered, rolling her eyes. "Now we'll have to hear about what a great gun person she is along with every thing else she brags about."

"You wish."

B.J. glanced at Cairn's face and found him looking at her, a look of bemused pride on his face. She smiled, showing no sign that her heart was slowly breaking.

"Let me try," she said.

He handed her the gun, and at the same time caught the faintest whiff of roses. His body stirred, and his famous ability to concentrate under the worst of battlefield conditions took a severe and unexpected beating. Instead of weaponry, he thought of sleek, warm skin, and the candlelight playing over a beautiful woman's face. Instead of trajectory and load, he remembered the soft little moans she made in her throat as her pleasure built.

While he showed her how to remove the spent shells and load anew, he was far too aware of the smooth, ripe breasts only inches from his hands.

"Like this?" she murmured, glancing up. Instead of checking her stance, he found himself watching her mouth, so ready to kiss her it hurt. "Not quite," he said gruffly, adjusting her hold.

"Okay?" She, too, seemed to be having trouble with her concentration. Instead of sighting on the imaginary target, she seemed preoccupied with his face, her eyes soft and luminous.

"Fine." He had to clear his throat suddenly. Angry at the world, furious with God or the cosmos or whatever fate had made it impossible to stay with her, he stepped back, nodding at her to fire when ready.

From the corner of his eye, he saw Emily and Ardeth huddled over a snapshot in Emily's hand, while Ricky tried to get a peek. Probably a dirty picture, he thought, remembering Ardeth's interest in the *Playboy* centerfold.

The gun went off suddenly, and B.J. grinned, her face as flushed as a bride's. "Once you get used to the noise, it's not so bad."

Like dying, he thought as he took the gun from her and returned it to the shed. Once you got used to the idea, it wasn't too scary. Just damn infuriating.

He emerged to find the girls closer. "Uh, Mom? Cairn? Can we talk to you a minute? It's kinda important."

Murdock met her puzzled gaze for an instant before they turned toward the girls. "Sure," B.J. told her daughters with a smile. "But what's with the solemn faces?"

Not only were they solemn, she realized, but their entire bodies were still as statues, only their eyes moving, staring first at Cairn and then at her. "Ardie? Em? What's wrong?"

Emily took a deep breath. "We're not sure."

"Pretty sure," Ardeth added quickly, glancing at her sister. "Show them the picture."

Emily stepped forward, a small color snapshot trembling slightly in her hand. "I found this in the small trunk upstairs, the one with your high school and college stuff," she told her mother in a too-quiet voice.

"We think this is a picture of you and our real father on your wedding day," Ardeth added in an equally subdued tone.

B.J. took the photo reluctantly, already sure she knew what she would see. Cairn looked so handsome and strong in his whites, standing next to his impossibly young bride.

"Let me see, Mommy. I wanna see, too." Ricky pulled her hand down to his eye level.

"That's you," he said, pleased at his own brilliance. "And that man there, that's Cairn, right?"

B.J. smiled. "Yes," she said softly, her eyes filling with tears she wouldn't let herself shed. "That's Cairn."

Silently she handed Murdock the picture.

Taking it was a mistake. Because then he had to look into the face of his bride again, and the pure joy he saw there almost tore him in two. She'd been so happy, so trusting, so openly in love. In five short years he'd managed to grind it all into dust.

As he glanced up into the faces of the daughters she'd given him, there was a pressure in his chest that he couldn't seem to swallow away, and his face felt numb.

"So now that you know, how do you feel about it?" he asked, his voice low and guarded.

Emily bit her lip and looked at her sister. Ardeth seemed acutely ill at ease. "Mom said you agreed to let Daddy—

Roger—adopt us because you knew it would be better for us to have only one dad."

"Your mom's right." His throat was so tight he had to force out the words.

Ricky tugged on B.J.'s hand, reminding her that she had three children whose world would never be the same after this moment. "What's Ardie talking about, Mommy?"

"About loving someone enough to do what's right for them instead of what you want to do."

"You mean like offering to share the last can of cream soda with your bestest friend in the whole wide world when you really want it all to yourself?"

B.J. smiled. "Exactly."

"Oh." Looking disappointed, Ricky released her hand and wandered off toward the house.

Murdock had never felt so awkward in his life. Not even when his arms and legs had seemed too long for the rest of him, and his voice had had a tendency to squeak at the worst possible times. It seemed natural to look to B.J. for help. Her smile had a way of smoothing jagged edges and shoring up his ragged confidence.

"I want you both to know that I asked Cairn not to tell you the truth," she told the girls with only the barest wobble to her voice. "He...can't stay permanently, and I didn't want you to be upset when he left."

Alarm sprang into Emily's eyes. "But you can't leave now!" she said to her newly found father. "Not when we're just getting used to having you here every day bossing us around."

"Em's right," Ardeth insisted, her voice more like her mother's than ever. "Daughters need their fathers, all the books say so."

"Yeah, and what about Mom? She needs you, too. Don't you, Mom?"

B.J. felt the tears gathering behind her eyes. "Don't push, darling. Cairn can't stay, and that's final. Let's not make him feel guilty because he has to go."

"But—"

"Em, please."

Something in her mother's tone must have gotten to her, because the belligerent expression left her face, and her eyes turned thoughtful. "Okay, but we can still call him 'Dad' while he's here, can't we?"

"That's up to him, I think."

Emily took the hint and directed her gaze toward Murdock. "Cairn? Is that all right with you?"

Murdock looked from one to the other, and simply nodded. At the moment speech was beyond him.

Emily beamed. "Terrific...Dad." She launched herself at him for a fierce hug, kissing him soundly on his cheek before letting go. Ardeth was more reserved.

"I'd rather call you 'Father,' if that's all right." Without waiting for an answer, she stepped into his arms and let him hug her for a long time. When he finally released her, tears were streaming down her cheeks, but the smile she gave him touched him deeply.

"Uh, is it okay if I tell Gary? About you being our father, I mean?"

Sensing the battle he was fighting for composure, B.J. answered for him. "It's up to you, honey."

"Then I will." She touched her hair, then looked at her watch. "Oh my gosh, he'll be here in three hours. I have to get ready." With that she turned and raced toward the house, only to stop at the edge of the shed to beckon to her sister. "Come *on*, Em. You promised to help me choose an outfit."

"It'll cost you!"

"Brat!"

The two raced toward the house, giggling.

Murdock slowly exhaled. "That wasn't as bad as it could be."

B.J. shook her head. "It wasn't bad at all."

"I need to hold you," he said, his tone raw. Without hesitation, she went into his arms, her own arms wrapping tightly around his lean middle. He held her tightly, his chin resting against her forehead. His body was tense, his muscles tight, and she knew he had to be struggling with emotions that he'd never allowed to surface before now.

So was she, she realized. Feelings of fierce pride at her daughters' utter willingness to accept a man they might reasonably be expected to resent mixed with utter despair because she knew that when he left, they would never see him again. It hurt so much. Like a dozen knives slowly skinning her sliver by sliver.

But when he held her away and looked down into her face, she managed a bright smile. "So, Dad, how do *you* feel now?"

"About ten feet tall, for starters," he admitted, his mouth softening briefly into a smile of his own. "I know I shouldn't say it, but, damn, I love you."

She took a deep breath, desperate to force back sudden hot tears. She failed.

"Oh, God, Cairn, I love you, too. I don't want you to die."

Her tears were like salt on a newly opened wound, and the faint tremble of her lips had him wanting to rage. Gently, because he didn't feel gentle, he held her at a distance, far enough so that he could kiss the tears from her lashes.

"Don't, baby, please don't. Help me do what I have to do."

He kissed her deeply, gently, and when he at last lifted his head again, she somehow found the strength to smile through her tears.

"Come on, Commander. Get that gun out again, and let me shoot it for real this time. Just in case."

Eleven

————

It was a sniper's moon. Silver-dollar full, it cast enough light to allow Murdock to read the face of his watch. Just as he figured, it was going on three, the time when a man's body was at its lowest ebb. For that reason, most ambushes were planned for that hour.

His own body was wired, ready for action. For once he felt almost normal—or as normal as it got these days. At least his head didn't hurt, and his vision was decent.

As he'd promised Hayden Tremaine, he'd given him until midnight. When he hadn't heard from the old man by then, he'd figured he'd been had. It disappointed him. It didn't surprise him.

From his vantage point in a clump of bushes near the hedge roses he could surveil the pump house on one side and the lane on the other. Turning his head, but not his body, he sighted on the spot across the river where he figured they'd park if they came again.

So far, there'd been no sign of trouble. The air was still, and nothing moved. Even the deer that usually came to the river to drink had taken shelter.

Since Gary had brought Ardeth home from the fair a little past midnight, the house had been quiet. Only one light burned, the one in B.J.'s bedroom. He let his mind linger on an image of her tucked into bed, still rosy and warm from her bath, waiting for him to come to her.

His body went from braced to aroused at the thought. He enjoyed the feeling for a long moment, then shut himself down until his mind was focused on the mission and his blood had cooled.

He heard the muted drone of a vehicle on the lane a split second before he saw its headlights. Someone was coming toward the house. It didn't seem logical that they would risk a frontal assault, not if a combat-trained man like Sarge were in charge. Still, nothing was impossible.

As soon as he recognized Gary's truck, he broke cover and jogged toward it. The boy was already out of the cab and racing pell-mell toward the cabin when Murdock called his name. They met near the oak.

"I heard them talking," Gary explained, wild-eyed. "When I got home from the fair."

"Be specific. Who was talking?"

Murdock's calm seemed to steady the boy. "Dad and Sarge Crookshank and a bunch of other guys I've seen around the mill yard." He paused to gulp air. "Dad laid off two shifts this morning. Didn't even give them any notice. They're really mad this time, Cairn, and Dad's just egging them on, talking about how he didn't have a choice, how it was Mrs. Dalton's fault, not his. How someone should do something about her before it's too late."

"Where were these guys when you heard all this?"

"At the mill."

"I thought you said you were at home."

"I was, at first. See, Granddad was at my house when I got there, waiting to talk to Dad about something important. The trees, I think. Anyway, the two of us kinda hung around talking, but I could see Granddad was really getting ticked off 'cause Dad hadn't come home, so I offered to drive him to the mill."

"Why the mill?"

"Sometimes Dad sleeps on the couch in his office if he's been working late."

Murdock nodded. "Go on."

"Okay, so Dad was there, only down in the yard by the shipping pallets." Gary drew a hasty breath. "It's like Dad was a different person, crazy like. Passing around a bottle of Jack Daniel's, talking wild." His expression turned beseeching. "Maybe he was drunk, you know? Maybe when he sleeps it off, he'll be his old self again."

"What about your grandfather?"

"Funny thing, as soon as he saw what was happening, he got all coldlike. Said he was going to try and talk some sense into Dad and the others, but just in case, I should come out and warn you."

Murdock grunted approval. "Okay, you run up to the house. The doors should be locked, so bang as loud as you can. When Mrs. Dalton answers, tell her what you told me and ... *damn it to hell!*"

Two vehicles were creeping up the lane, using only parking lights.

"That's Sarge's pickup in front!" Gary cried, looking panicked. "Oh Lord, Mr. Murdock, some of those guys had rifles! And they were talking about burning the house."

"Calm down, son. We'll handle it. Tell Mrs. Dalton to load the shotgun, with real shot this time, but she's to stay in the house unless someone gets past me. Then she's to take the kids and head for the river. They'll be safe on the other side. Got that?"

"Yessir."

"Good. Get moving!" Murdock gave the boy a shove, and he took off running.

Senses sharpened, Murdock slipped his automatic from his boot, then melted into the shadows behind the pin oak's huge trunk. He figured they'd go for the cabin first. When they did, they'd find a reception committee of one waiting.

B.J. slammed down the phone and grabbed her jeans. Hayden Tremaine had sounded shocked but rational. Something about a layoff, a plan of Garson's that had gotten out of hand. He'd already alerted the sheriff, who was on his way.

"Stall if you can," he'd warned. "If you can't, do exactly what Murdock tells you. Garson and I will be there as soon as we can."

A mob, he'd said. Out of control and primed for blood. Hers, her kids', Cairn's.

Later she would be furious. Now she had to remain in control. No matter what, the kids had to be protected.

Someone was pounding on the front door, startling her into action.

"Mrs. Dalton? Ardie? Wake up!" It was Gary's voice.

Grabbing a shirt, she pulled it over her head as she raced into the hall and down the steps. Gary started explaining as soon as she got the door open, but she cut him off.

"Your granddad just called. We have to get the kids up and dressed." She hurried back upstairs with Gary at her heels.

"Mr. Murdock said to get the shotgun, but stay in the house."

Terror gripped her at the thought of Cairn facing a mob alone. "Where is he?" she threw over her shoulder.

"Waiting for them outside."

"Oh no!" She stumbled on the top step and nearly fell. Slow down, she told herself. *Think*. What would Cairn do?

"Gary, get Ricky up and dressed," she ordered, indicating with her hand which room was his. "I'll get the girls."

"Gotcha." He disappeared into Ricky's bedroom.

Emily's room was at the end, and the door was closed. Throwing it open, she yelled for Emily to wake up, then crossed the hall and opened Ardeth's door.

"I thought I heard Gary." Ardeth was already sitting up in bed, looking scared and sleepy.

"You did. He came to warn us. There's going to be trouble. You need to get dressed right now!"

From Ricky's room she could hear the sound of Gary's voice as he coaxed the little boy into his clothes. Hearing nothing from Emily, she returned to her daughter's room and flipped on the light.

"Em, get up!"

"Mom?" Emily opened her eyes and peered through a groggy haze toward the door. Waking quickly had always been impossible for her second-born.

"Get dressed," B.J. ordered over the pounding of her heart. "There's trouble."

"Trouble?" Emily was up and stumbling, still half-asleep. B.J. hurried to the closet and pulled out a pair of jeans and a shirt.

"Here, put these on, and then get downstairs. If you see anyone coming toward the house besides Cairn or me, get your sister and brother and hightail it to the river. You'll be safe there if they try to burn us out."

Emily blinked at her, suddenly wide-awake and scared. "What are you going to do?"

"The first thing I'm going to do is load the shotgun. And then I'm going to pray I have the guts to use it."

The gun was in her closet on the top shelf, along with a sack of shells. Trying to will herself calm, she dropped the gun and shells on her bed, found her sneakers and shoved her feet into them as quickly as she could. Her hands were shaking so badly she had trouble tying the laces.

Gary was waiting for her when she got to the head of the stairs, still trying to push extra shells into the pocket of her jeans. Ardeth was there too, holding Ricky by the hand. Her son looked mussed, sleepy and annoyed.

"Mommy, Gary woke me up and made me get dressed and it's not even light outside!"

"I know, sweets. Just try to be patient, okay?" She ruffled his hair, but her gaze was on the front door. Snug in the crook of her arm, the now loaded shotgun felt cold and heavy.

"How many were there?" she asked Gary in a low tone.

"I saw two pickups. I don't know how many men, but I counted at least six at the mill."

She drew a deep breath. "Six against two," she said, holding the shotgun tighter.

"Three," Gary said firmly, clattering down the stairs. Reaching bottom, he jerked open the door. Instantly the sound of angry male voices filled their ears.

"Gary, wait!" Ardeth called, leaving Ricky to run down behind him. "Don't go! You might get hurt." She flung her arms around him and held on tight.

"I have to," he said, pulling her arms from his neck. "Mr. Murdock's all alone out there."

"Oh God!" Ardeth whispered. Whirling, she made eye contact with her mother coming down the stairs. "I'm going, too!"

"Me, too," Emily cried, following her mother.

"Absolutely not!"

"He's my father!" Ardeth exclaimed, looking frantic. "He'll be killed. All of you will be killed!"

B.J. saw the horror in her daughter's eyes and laid a none-too-steady hand on her shoulder. "No one's going to be killed. Once they see your mom and her trusty shotgun, they'll run for the hills."

"Mom! This is no time for jokes!" Emily protested.

"No, it's time to stay calm and do what your father says. And he wants you both to stay here and take care of your brother." Before either of the girls could protest, she went on, speaking quickly. "Ardie, you watch the back of the house, Em, watch the front. The sheriff's on his way, and so are Gary's dad and grandfather. Keep the doors locked, and the inside lights out."

"But—"

"Just do it, girls. I'm counting on you both." Trusting to Ardeth's good sense, if not Emily's, she followed Gary onto the porch.

The full moon illuminated the yard, but the shouts and telltale sounds of a scuffle came from the sheltered area beneath the oak where two trucks were parked side by side, their parking lights casting a dim glow. All four doors were open, as though men had piled out in a rush. She could see shadows and shapes merging and separating in a distorted dance of violence.

In the distance she heard the shrill wail of a siren, then another, and her hopes soared. This time the cavalry wasn't going to be too late.

She and Gary were halfway down the steps when four shots rang out, followed by two more in quick succession. B.J. clutched the heavy gun and ran toward the sound.

Gary was faster and sped past her, only to disappear into the shadows. There was a shout, a cry and then another burst of gunfire. By the time she was close enough to see what was happening, two men were on the ground, lying inert. A third was down on one knee, his head hanging and his chest heaving. She thought he was gripping a rifle.

Murdock was coldly furious. At himself, mostly.

Someone else had been driving Sarge's truck. That same someone must have left the ex-Marine across the river before continuing to the farm. While Murdock had been talking with Gary, Sarge had crossed the river, timing his arrival with the appearance of the trucks.

Five men had gotten out, three of them carrying rifles. As soon as Murdock ordered them to get back in the truck and leave, one had snapped off a couple of quick shots in the direction of his voice.

Murdock had managed to take out two of the arsonists before Sarge jumped him from behind. At the same time two other guys hit him from the front.

Four months ago he would have cracked some heads and gotten himself out of trouble. Now he had trouble holding his own.

Even full out, using all his tricks, he lost the gun to the biggest of the lot. Sarge, he thought, before survival took all of his attention.

B.J. spotted Murdock grappling with two men while Gary rode the back of another holding a handgun. He turned to the light and she recognized Sarge Crookshank, his face twisted with hate as he tried to buck Gary free.

Just as she opened her mouth to shout at them to stop, Cairn dug an elbow into the gut of one of his assailants. At the same time he clipped the other man with a kick to the knee. Both recoiled in obvious pain. One went down, but the other recovered enough to land a punch to Murdock's jaw. Cairn's head snapped back, and he staggered but somehow kept his footing.

Meanwhile, the man who had been kneeling got to his feet. B.J. saw the rifle then, held by the barrel like a club. He was behind Murdock, out of his line of sight.

"Cairn, watch out!" she shouted, but it was too late. The rifle butt connected with the back of his head, pitching him forward. Somehow he managed to ram, linebacker fashion, into Sarge's belly.

Both men went down, Sarge taking Gary with him. The gun went off, and she screamed.

In the distance the sirens changed pitch, grew louder. The others heard the same wail, shouting at one another to "get the hell out." With an enraged bellow, Sarge surged to his feet, the gun in his hand only inches from Cairn's head.

"If I go, you do too, you bastard," he snarled, clearly beyond reason.

Sobbing, terrified, B.J. pointed the shotgun at Sarge's back and pulled both triggers. With a deafening roar, the gun jerked upward, and she stumbled backward, landing on her backside.

Right that moment, the sheriff's car screeched to a halt and two men piled out, guns drawn. No more than an instant later the fire department rescue van and two trucks pulled into the circle, their lights turning the scene into a nightmarish tangle of bodies and blood.

Radios squawked static, voices shouted, someone cursed. Firemen and deputies went about their business, bringing order to chaos.

By the time she scrambled to her feet and reached Murdock's side, one of the EMTs already had his shirt open, applying CPR while the other tended Gary, who was bleeding profusely from a shoulder wound.

Shaking violently, she sank to her knees next to Cairn, willing him to survive. Blood was pooling under his head from a gash near the hairline and his skin was eerily pale in the moonlight. His hands were covered with blood from the raw knuckles, and his lip had been split. She was sobbing hysterically as she brushed the hair away from his bruised face. He didn't move, and fear stabbed her heart.

"Damn you, Cairn Murdock," she whispered brokenly through her tears, "Don't you dare leave us. Don't you dare!"

Though well-equipped and up-to-date medically, Myrtle Community Hospital had only a tiny waiting room outside the OR. Every chair was occupied.

B.J. and her girls sat on one side, staring at nothing, speaking only in monosyllables. Ricky was spending the night with Bernice Coats who, as soon as the word spread about the attack, had been the first to offer B.J. her apologies—and her help.

On the other side of the room sat the Tremaines, father and son. The sixth chair was occupied by Gary's mother. Frances Tremaine and B.J. had known each other casually, the way mothers do when their children run in the same social crowd.

Frances had relinquished custody of her son to Garson after the divorce, because, as she'd told B.J. at the time, a boy needed a strong role model in his life. B.J. wondered now if she was having second thoughts.

Clearly wrenched from bed by the news, she was wearing mismatched workout sweats and her face was scrubbed and bare. Somewhere along the line, she'd run a comb through her hair and pulled it back with a rubber band.

She and B.J. had exchanged hugs when she'd arrived, and Frances had asked after the children. B.J. had assured her they were safe before the tears had clogged her throat.

Cairn had still been unconscious but breathing on his own when they'd loaded him into the van. It was only then she'd found out he'd taken a bullet in the side. Gary had been shaken, but conscious and lucid. Both were now in surgery.

"Mr. and Mrs. Tremaine?"

The man in the sweat-stained scrubs looked too young to be a surgeon—until B.J. saw his eyes. They were far older than his facial features suggested. At the moment, they were bloodshot from weariness, but he was smiling.

Ardeth clutched her mother's arm, her eyes pleading with the doctor for good news. Noticing, he sent her an encouraging look before concentrating his attention on Gary's family.

Garson and Frances shot to their feet at the same time. It took Hayden a moment longer.

"How is he, Doctor?" Garson rasped.

"Your son tolerated the surgery well, and it looks as though the bullet did only temporary damage. He's young and healthy and from all indications should recover fully."

"Thank God." Frances leaned against her former husband for a long moment, her throat working and her eyes tightly closed. Pale and shaken, Garson put his arm around her and patted her shoulder awkwardly.

He and his father had arrived at the farm as the EMTs were preparing to wheel Gary to the van. Since then, he had seemed numb, his face ravaged and his eyes vacant. Now they took on a semblance of life.

"When can we see him?" he demanded almost rudely.

"Not until he's out of recovery. Another hour at least."

Hayden drew in a ragged breath, then let it out slowly. "We are most grateful to you, sir," he told the young surgeon with great dignity.

"As we are grateful to you, Mr. Tremaine, for your generous donations to the hospital over the years." His face relaxed, becoming even more boyish. "In fact, you might even take some of the credit for saving your grandson's life."

Hayden swallowed hard, and his eyes brimmed with tears. "Thank you for that. It means a lot."

"You're welcome."

He turned to leave, only to stop when B.J. leapt to her feet. "Doctor, about my ... Mr. Murdock?"

"He's still in surgery."

She nodded, her body feeling as though it were made of wood. The doctor's eyes crinkled, but his expression remained sober.

"Dr. Cabot's a world-class surgeon. I've seen him pull off more than one miracle."

He left as quickly as he'd come, leaving the room charged with new energy. B.J. stood frozen, watching Garson ease his ex-wife into her chair. Straightening, he turned to face B.J. again, his expression conciliatory.

"B.J.—"

"Don't bother with false apologies," she told him wearily. "Just be glad your son is going to be all right." She hesitated, then added with more spirit. "While you're at it, be proud he's more of a man at sixteen than you'll ever be."

He flinched, his gaze darting to his father briefly before returning to her face. "Crookshank swore there'd be no guns involved. He swore they would just make a lot of noise and pretend they were going to burn the house unless you agreed to sell. I know how much that old place means to you, more than the trees, I suspect. I figured you'd realize that sooner or later. I just wanted it to be sooner."

"And you trusted a man like Sarge Crookshank to keep his word?" she asked incredulously.

Garson turned a sickly red. "No," he said very softly. "I knew they'd burn the place, but I swear to you, B.J.—" he turned to look at his father again, this time beseechingly "—I swear to both of you I didn't think anyone would be hurt."

"You didn't think," Hayden corrected in the coldest voice B.J. had ever heard. "What's more, you lied to me when you said you knew nothing about that first arson attack, and you lied to your son when you told him you were going to settle this peacefully." The old man's control faltered, and he took a moment to compose himself before shifting his gaze to B.J.

"You have my word, my dear. No one at Cascade Timber will ever try to coerce you into doing anything against your will. Whatever you decide about the trees, the money Garson offered you is yours, no strings attached."

She felt a lump in her throat. "Thank you for the offer, Hayden, but right now the money, the trees, nothing matters but the man who saved our lives. And if he dies..."

She couldn't finish.

Hayden hesitated, then put his arm around her shoulder and pulled her close. She rested her cheek against the lapel of his tweed jacket and thought about her grandfather. He'd buried two wives and four children on the land that was hers now, somewhere in the woods that she'd tried so hard to protect.

"Mom?" Emily touched her arm, drawing her gaze. "Ardie and I are going down the hall to the machine for sodas. Can we bring you some coffee or soup or something?"

B.J. smiled her thanks. "I couldn't swallow a thing, but you go ahead."

"Mrs. Tremaine, would you like something?" Emily asked politely.

"Coffee," Frances murmured, "if it's no trouble."

"Do you have enough money?" Hayden asked gruffly.

Emily nodded. Both she and her sister offered their mother encouraging looks before they left the room.

Garson cleared his throat. "Guess I was wrong about Gary and your oldest, B.J. Sorry about that."

It was the cavalier look to his smile that made her snap. That, and the resurgence of confidence that seemed to have taken him over again.

Very carefully, she stepped from Hayden's comforting arms and straightened her spine. Then with as much force as she could muster, she drew back her arm, doubled her fist and punched Garson in the nose.

Something crunched, and he let out a howl of pain. Blood trickled from one nostril, and his nose was already ballooning.

"Why you little bitch!" he snarled, his intention to retaliate in kind obvious.

His father stepped between them, his face livid. "Enough, Garson! Don't make things any worse for yourself."

"Me? What about her, the hypocritical tramp!"

B.J. gasped, but Hayden laid a warning hand on her shoulder before turning to square off against his son.

"I never thought I would have occasion to say this to you or anyone carrying Tremaine blood, but you've left me no choice. I'm deeply ashamed of you, Garson, and if I have anything to say about it, you will never make decisions for Cascade Timber again."

Shock burst in the younger man's eyes, and the flush faded from his skin until it was pasty gray. At his sides, his hands opened and closed spasmodically.

"You can't do that to me," he said in a strangled voice. "I'm all the family you have."

"You forget Gary. Someday he'll be old enough to run Cascade, and I just might hang on long enough to see that day. In the meantime, I know of one or two excellent men who can act in his stead. I might even take over again myself."

Rage shimmered in Garson's yellow eyes as he swiped away the blood. "I'll fight you, old man. I swear I will."

One side of Hayden's mouth twitched. "You're forgetting one more thing, Garson. You broke the law by inciting Crookshank and the others into violence. Assault and battery, attempted arson—the sheriff tells me he's got a long list of charges and enough evidence to back them up."

"That's absurd! Orrin Beaver is one of my best friends. He knows better than to try something like that."

Hayden looked suddenly sad. "Your mother always said I was spoiling you by not making you work for the things I gave you. To my eternal shame, she was right."

Garson's face twisted. "Screw you, and her, too," he shouted before bolting from the room. At the door he nearly collided with a large man in scrubs.

B.J. knew immediately that this was Cairn's surgeon. And he wasn't smiling.

Twelve

___

Everything in the ICU was high-tech and sterile. Monitors, IVs, tubes and wires—all to keep Cairn alive. B.J. was almost accustomed to the beeps and clicks as the equipment functioned flawlessly.

It had been nearly twenty-four hours since he'd come out of surgery. Every hour she or one of the girls was allowed to sit by his bed for five minutes. So far he hadn't stirred.

"Won't be long now before he wakes up," the nurse said, checking the heart monitor. "His breathing has changed, and his heart rate is stronger. This morning he was thrashing around pretty good. Reminded me of a swimmer fighting his way to the surface."

B.J. swallowed the sick feeling in her throat and managed a wan smile. "He was a SEAL. Maybe he was dreaming."

The nurse gave her an encouraging smile. "Don't tell Dr. Cabot I said so, but I'd just about guarantee this one is going to make it. He has that look about him." Her grin widened. "I'll bet he's pretty tough to handle when he's wide-awake and feeling good."

"You've got that right." Her voice caught, and she bit her lip. "Sorry. It's just that this waiting is so hard."

The nurse's smile faded. "Trust me, it won't be long." She glanced at her watch, then at the door. "Officially your five minutes are up, but my watch has been known to be wrong before. Just don't tell anyone I told you that, okay?"

"I'll be quiet as a mouse."

"What mouse?" The nurse was chuckling to herself as she left the cubicle.

Now that she was alone again, the silence seemed deafening. Even the routine noises of the equipment were welcome.

"Everything's going to be just fine, my darling," she murmured, pressing the big hand she held to her cheek. His knuckles were swollen and bruised, and several had been sutured where the skin had split.

Lovingly she let her gaze rest on Cairn's battered face. One eye was nearly swollen shut, and the skin surrounding it had turned a rich, deep purple. The bridge of his nose had been rearranged, and his lip was cut.

He had a severe concussion, the doctor had explained, and twenty stitches in the back of his head. The bullet that had hit him in the side had nicked his pelvic bone, then exited cleanly. It had been the sliver of shrapnel in Cairn's brain that had had Dr. Cabot alarmed.

Upon learning all that B.J. could tell him, he'd called Dr. Frundt at Bethesda, who had expressed him a copy of Cairn's medical record. It was then that she'd learned of the operation that almost surely would save Cairn's life.

"The girls and Ricky and I took a vote," she murmured softly. "We're not going to let you leave us."

He didn't respond.

"Mrs. Dalton?"

B.J. jerked awake at the sound of her name and tried to will herself alert. Through a fog of exhaustion she saw the night nurse bending over her.

"What time is it?" Her neck was stiff from trying to sleep curled up in a chair, and her mouth was dry.

"Just past eleven. Mr. Murdock is asking for you." She snorted. "More like ordered me to find you 'on the damned double.'"

"Awake? Cairn's awake?" Somehow she managed to force the words out coherently.

"I'll say! The man's impossible already."

Overjoyed, B.J. scrambled to her feet and all but skipped after the nurse through the double doors into the ICU.

He seemed to be sleeping when she entered the cubicle. But the moment she touched his hand he opened his eyes and looked at her.

"'Bout time they let you in," he managed hoarsely.

"Hey, don't give them any trouble, okay? As a favor to me?"

Murdock wanted to tell her he'd do any damn thing she asked of him. Instead he tried for a smile and discovered his face was numb.

"The kids?" he asked.

"Fine. They said to give Dad their love."

He pulled in enough air to keep himself steady. "What, no kisses for the old man?"

B.J.'s smile wobbled. "Lots of them." She had to lower the side of the bed first, then bent over to kiss him very gently on his bruised mouth.

"That's from Ricky," she murmured, her mouth only inches from his. "This one's from Em." She kissed him again, then murmured, "And this is from Ardie."

He tried to lift his hand to touch her hair, but his arms were too heavy. Instead he closed his eyes and let himself breathe in the scent of roses. When he found himself drifting into sleep again, he forced his eyes open so that he could concentrate on her face.

"Aren't you forgetting someone?" he asked when she straightened again.

She linked her fingers with his. Keep it light, she told herself. No hysterics, no begging. When he's stronger we'll talk about the operation.

"Hmm, let me think a minute."

His eyebrows bunched ominously. "Think later. Give me a kiss, damn it, while I can still keep my eyes open to enjoy it."

This time she smoothed his hair away from his face before she kissed him. This time she let her lips linger on his before, regretfully, she straightened again.

"How's that?"

His lashes fluttered. "Terrific," he murmured. "Want more."

"Later," she whispered. "You need to rest."

His mouth quirked. "As soon as you tell me what happened."

B.J. remembered her vow to keep it light. Telling him about Gary could wait until later. "Let's see. Hayden fired Garson, which was pretty much for the best since he's probably going to jail for a while, if you can believe the newspapers."

He looked pleased at that. "Did I shoot someone?"

"Two someones. Both survived."

"Sarge?"

B.J. dropped her gaze to their entwined hands. "He's in jail."

"You sound like you're sorry."

Her head came up and her eyes flashed. "He was going to shoot you! I had a perfect bead on his backside. Couldn't miss in fact."

Murdock fought to keep awake. "What...happened?"

"I was afraid you'd ask me that."

Beneath the covers his chest was bare, and she let her fingertips rest lightly on his shoulder. His skin was warm, but no longer burning with fever. Glancing at his face again, she saw a smile come into his deep gray eyes, and she wanted to fall to her knees in gratitude.

"Tell me," he ordered gruffly.

She took a resigned breath. "I loaded the damn gun with blanks by mistake, and when it went off, the only thing that got hit was my backside when I ended up sitting on a rock."

It took a minute to settle in, but when it did, he couldn't keep from laughing. Which was a bad mistake, because his body immediately reminded him that he'd been shot. When he couldn't quite stifle a groan, B.J. panicked.

"Cairn? Are you all right? Should I call the nurse?"

He tightened his fingers as much as he could and shook his head. "Okay, now," he said when the worst of the pain eased.

"You scared me," she said, her mouth far too pale and her eyes too bright.

"Sorry." His lashes drooped, and it took great effort to keep his eyes from closing completely. "Go home and get some sleep," he ordered. "Kiss my kids for me, all three of them."

"I will," she whispered as he fell asleep.

She left reluctantly. But the fear that had gripped her since she'd arrived at the hospital was ebbing. At the door she turned to look at him one more time. He didn't know it yet, but he was going to have that operation.

As soon as he was out of ICU, he'd been told about Gary, and the two of them had ended up sharing a room. Because of that, she and Cairn were never alone.

The girls visited every afternoon, becoming more and more attached to their father. B.J. visited every night.

During several visits when she and Hayden found themselves visiting at the same time, they came to an agreement about her woods. Instead of clear-cutting, Cascade's loggers would harvest only selected trees, perhaps one in four, using judicious methods—horses instead of dozers, helicopters instead of trucks.

Part of the money Garson had offered would go to a fund Hayden was setting up to retrain unemployed timber workers. Both she and Hayden considered it a fair compromise.

Murdock and Gary agreed. The girls were glad to have the whole thing settled, and the phone began ringing night and day with calls from friends who wanted to make up. Ricky's feelings were a lot simpler. He wanted his new daddy home where he belonged.

On the sixth day, Gary was discharged into his mother's care, and B.J. made up her mind to bring up the subject of the operation that evening. All day she practiced her arguments, trying to foresee Cairn's objections and forming logical rebuttals.

Even so, when she arrived with a plate of snicker doodles that Emily had made just for him, and a fresh bouquet of roses from the garden, she found herself scared to death.

"So what else did you bring me?" he asked with a grin that seemed to come easier each time she showed up.

"This," she murmured, leaning over to kiss him so thoroughly they were both breathing hard when it ended.

"Very nice," he drawled, his gaze dropping to the swell of her breasts. "In fact..." He cupped her breast with his hand and wiggled his eyebrows. "I think I feel an urge coming on."

"Don't even think about it, Murdock," she teased, swatting his hand away. "And scoot over, so I can sit down."

"With the greatest of pleasure, sweetheart. Want me to make it easier for you and strip down, too?"

The thought of lying next to his naked body again had her heart racing. But that would have to wait. "I said 'sit.' Nothing more."

He muttered something pithy, and she couldn't help grinning. "Behave yourself. There's something we need to discuss."

Murdock saw the determination in her eyes and knew the next few minutes were going to be rough for both of them. He had a hunch she knew about the operation and wanted to talk about it with him. Argue was more like it, he decided, watching her chin tilt and her lips set in the stubborn little line that meant business.

He had half a mind to stop her with a kiss, which he was pretty sure he could stretch into as much lovemaking as two people could manage in a hospital room with limited privacy. Much as the thought tantalized him, he knew he'd only be prolonging the inevitable.

Even so, as she settled against his shoulder, he couldn't quite keep from stealing a quick kiss. "You taste good," he said, touching his tongue to her lower lip and receiving a melting smile in return.

"Stop trying to distract me," she murmured, but her eyes were soft.

"Then stop flirting with me."

"I don't flirt, remember?" She nipped his chin with her teeth, and he pretended to be annoyed. She wasn't fooled.

"You're beginning to look like your old handsome self," she murmured. "Except for that new bump on your nose."

Desire was beginning to thrum through him, but he tamped it down. Holding her, being on the receiving end of that impish sense of humor was more healing than any of the drugs they'd pumped into him. And when she left him at night, he missed her so much he had trouble falling asleep. It was embarrassing to admit, even to himself, just how crazy he was about her.

"My daughters like the new me."

"That's because they think you're just about perfect."

His gut twisted. "I'll miss them when I'm gone."

B.J. froze, then slowly drew away from him until she could see his face clearly. Her own had gone pale. "Gone? But you can't leave now. Not now."

He made himself meet her disbelieving gaze head-on. "I don't have a choice. I wish I did."

The hope that sparked in her eyes nearly tore him in two. "But that's just it, you do! Dr. Cabot told me about the operation Captain Frundt recommended. As soon as you've recovered your strength, we'll go to Bethesda together."

Murdock felt himself shutting down, the way a man did when he went into battle. This time it wasn't as easy as it should be. He had a feeling a few more months around B.J. and her brood, and it would be damn near impossible. Perhaps that was what scared him the most.

"Did Cabot tell you I'd wake up blind from Frundt's precious operation?" He made his voice cold and hard, then flinched inwardly when hurt crept into her eyes.

"Yes, he told me. But you would be alive, and that's all that really matters."

"To you maybe," he said, trying to gentle his tone. "Not to me. I'd rather die right now than live a minute of my life in darkness."

She winced, her eyes flooding with sympathy. "I know it seems really terrible to you now, but this week, I've found out a lot about the new methods they have for helping the blind. Maybe it's not exactly a normal life, but it's pretty close. I made copies of the articles, and I'll—"

"Forget it." His voice was flat. Final. "There will be no operation. If you can't accept that, you might as well leave now because that's the last time I intend to discuss this with you or anyone."

B.J. stared at him, not wanting to believe him, but knowing that she had no choice. Hurt welled inside her until her chest felt tight and achy. Why hadn't she expected this? she thought, fighting an icy wave of nausea. If only she'd expected it, she wouldn't have felt so shattered.

"If you don't care enough about me to fight for your life, what about your children?" she challenged desperately, her control hanging by a thread. "Can you just walk away from them without a backward look?"

A muscle pulled along his jawline, but his expression remained unyielding. "You'd be surprised what a man without options can do."

B.J. wet her lips nervously, then drew a quick breath. "Look, we don't have to talk about this now. Dr. Cabot plans to release you tomorrow. Why don't we sleep on it, and tomorrow—"

"Tomorrow I'll be on a plane out of here."

Her jaw dropped, and her throat worked spasmodically. "I see."

Watching her struggle to control her shock took all of his strength. There was so much he wanted to tell her, so much she deserved to hear, but saying those things required more guts than he had left.

"Where... where are you going?"

"South Carolina first, to see my dad."

She nodded, as pale as the sheet. "Say hello for me, please. I always liked your f-father."

"B.J.—"

"No, I'm fine, Cairn. Really I am. I realize that your mind is made up, and since I know you never make a practice of compromising, I also realize there's nothing more I can say to change it."

She offered him a smile that almost seemed genuine. Unless the man receiving it was in love with her. Then he couldn't miss the slight wobble at the edges and the bruised look around her eyes.

"I'd stay if I could." Admitting that was more than he'd intended.

"Of course, you would. And that's exactly what I'll tell the children when they ask me why you won't be attending the welcome-home party they're so busy planning for their father."

He nearly lost it then. Only years of rigid discipline kept him from breaking down. "I'm sorry, B.J. I never wanted to hurt them. Or you."

He knuckled the tears from her cheek that he was positive she didn't know she was shedding. When she flinched, he dropped his hand, and braced himself for the punishment he knew he deserved.

"You saved our lives, Cairn. No matter what, we still love you for caring enough to come to us. We always will." She kissed his cheek very gently, then climbed from the bed. "Remember that when you go."

She picked up her purse, leaned down to inhale the perfume of the bright roses by his bed, then straightened her shoulders and gave him one last look.

"Perhaps you could drop us a postcard from time to time?"

"If you'd like." He cleared his throat. "You're listed in my personnel file as next of kin. And I never got around to changing my will. My attorney has your address and phone number."

B.J. felt as though she were drowning. Her chest was on fire, and her throat seemed to constrict tighter with each breath she took. "I...please don't tell me any more. I can't handle any more right now."

"Whatever you say."

She was shaking badly inside, and she was becoming lightheaded. "It's getting late. I'd better go." Her smile tore into him like poisoned talons. "Besides, if you're traveling tomorrow, you'll need your rest."

"Will I see you again before I go?" The question came from nowhere, surprising them both.

She shook her head slowly. "It's better that we say goodbye now."

A feeling akin to panic hit him full on. Before he had the sense to ask to see the kids one more time, she was at the door. "God bless you," she said, and then she was gone.

Cairn waited until the sound of her running footsteps faded before he reached up and turned off the light over his bed. In the semidarkness, his room seemed cold. Empty.

Like his life from this moment on, he thought as he pressed the button and lowered the bed. Lying flat, one arm over his eyes, he tried to bring his thoughts under control.

It was better this way. She and the kids would only suffer more the longer he was with them. They'd already buried one father. He was simply sparing them more heartache. So why the hell did he feel lower than a snake's belly at this particular moment?

Rigid, sick inside, he listened to the pounding of his heart, and the familiar sounds of a hospital settling in for the night. Mission accomplished, he thought. Time to move on.

Time to find that lonely mountaintop.

Closing his eyes he willed his mind to shut down. He'd set his course and he meant to keep to it. B.J. was right. Compromise wasn't in him.

And yet, maybe, just maybe it could be. After all, he'd taken two hard cracks to the skull and he was still alive. Maybe Frundt and the other two doctors he'd called in were wrong.

Turning on his side, he stared at the roses still faintly visible in the light from the hall. If he stayed, B.J. could teach him their names. And they could plant more, one for every year they had together. Rows and rows of beautiful roses for their grandchildren to see.

And in the spring he would make love to her with their perfume coming in the window on the breeze. In the summer they would water them in the early morning together, and then walk to the river together, planning their day.

Excitement built in his chest as he threw off the sheet and left the bed. If she was willing to take a chance, so was he.

He was just pulling on his boots when he heard a commotion in the hall, followed by the deceptively calm voice of the paging operator calling a "Code Blue" on his floor.

Like a well-executed military drill, a team of doctors and nurses converged on the room two doors down. In the corridor a woman and her two children, a boy and a girl, huddled together, sobbing.

Murdock stood frozen in the doorway, listening to the cruel sounds of resuscitation that seemed to go on and on. Then, it was over, and a man in a doctor's white coat came out to tell the already-grieving woman and her disbelieving children that her husband and their father was dead.

Like a man in a trance, Murdock collected the few belongings that had been in his pockets when he'd been brought in, took one last look at the bright, beautiful roses and walked out.

* * *

It was early when B.J. and the children arrived at the hospital. Like an army on the march, they headed straight for Murdock's room. It might not be fair to use the children as allies. It probably wasn't admirable, either. But sometime around four in the morning, she'd stopped weeping and started scheming. He might still leave them, but not until they'd used every weapon they had to keep him where he belonged.

Outside the room she came to a sudden halt. "Okay, you all know what you're going to say, right?"

"Right," the three of them chorused.

Emily, in particular, looked determined. "Leave it to us, Mom. Dad won't have a chance when we get started."

B.J. managed a smile, then pushed open the door. Both beds were empty. A janitor was scrubbing the floor. He looked up when they entered, a bored look on his weathered face.

"If you're looking for the man who's been here this past week, he's gone. Checked himself out last night slick as you please." His gaze shifted to the bedside tray. "Nurse said he took everything 'cept that there silver dollar."

It was then that B.J. realized just how much it hurt to lose the same man twice in a lifetime.

B.J. rested her back against the fir's thick trunk and let her eyes drift closed. It hadn't rained in two weeks, and the ground was finally dry. The air had warmed at last after a seemingly endless winter, and the smells of a newborn spring teased her nostrils.

Tomorrow Cascade's loggers would begin felling trees on Berryman land for the first time in over a century. The crew's foreman had already marked the first trees to be cut. The Douglas fir she was leaning against was one of them. Silly as it might seem to most people, she had come to the woods today to say her goodbyes to those trees.

Suddenly restless in spite of the serenity that usually soothed her, she drew up her legs and circled them with her arms. Resting her cheek on her knees, she thought back over the last nine months. Time enough to bring a baby into the world, she thought. Only that wasn't something she could do any more than she could forget the man she desperately wanted to give her that baby.

To no one's surprise Cairn had kept his promise. Postcards had come regularly during the first few months after he'd left. From South Carolina and Florida and the Bahamas. The last had come in January, postmarked New Hampshire. He'd found a place in the mountains, he'd written. Nothing fancy, but comfortable. So far there hadn't been much snow, but that was bound to change. He'd closed with love for all of them. Since then, nothing.

She didn't want to believe he was dead, but every day, when she fetched the mail, she was afraid she would find a letter from his attorney, telling her that he was.

A small shudder passed over her, leaving a dull ache in her chest. The pain of his leaving was less acute, but still a part of her. The girls, and particularly Ricky, still missed his steady presence in the fabric of their lives.

Emily had had copies made of the snapshot she'd found, and each of the children had one. B.J. kept hers next to the fresh white candle she'd placed by her bed. Every night, right before she turned out the light, she willed him to return to his family. Every morning when she left her bed, she told herself that today might be the day he came.

"After all, it's spring," she murmured to the majestic tree sheltering her. The breeze rustled the needles over her head, bringing the scent of budding flowers. It was a mix of sensations she always relished, but for the first time since she was a little girl, the peace she'd sought in the woods eluded her. The pain inside her was just too deep.

The last week in March was a busy one in Mantree. Garson Tremaine, Sarge Crookshank and their cohorts were found guilty of assault and sentenced to varying lengths of time in state prison. And Berryman Farm began hiring again.

On the first Monday after she'd put out the word, which just happened to be April Fools' Day, her yard was filled with so many familiar faces it seemed like a family reunion. Mike Feller had been the first in line, followed by Pedro Gomez and a goodly number of her old crew.

From dawn to well past midday, they'd come streaming up the lane. Some she'd put on immediately, others she took time to interview before hiring. A few she'd regrettably turned away. Tomorrow work would begin in earnest.

The sun was well past its zenith, and the late afternoon breeze was beginning to build by the time she was finally able to take a breather. Upstairs, Ricky and Trent were trying to come up with a good April fool's prank to pull on Emily and Ardeth when they returned from school. As the self-appointed referee of such things, B.J. had already rejected three of their notions, especially the one having to do with the garter snakes they'd been collecting for two days now.

Leaning back, she swirled the cubes in her glass of cream soda and thought about the busy days to come. From now until the end of autumn, she would have little time to do more than work and sleep and grab a quick bite to eat whenever she had a free moment. She might even be too exhausted to dream.

Her thoughts turned immediately to Cairn. One of these days she would stop missing him. Wouldn't she?

She took a sip, letting the icy soda slide down her throat. Somewhere nearby a jay squawked a warning, and a squirrel chimed in. Her faithful guardians, she thought, watching Patches and two of her nearly grown kittens playing tag among the rosebushes. When the jay called even more furiously a few moments later, she opened her tired eyes and looked lazily toward the road. A truck was pulling in the lane, one she didn't recognize.

Another job seeker, she thought, resigned to telling him that he was too late. Her crew was full.

She waited until he parked the truck next to hers, then she left her seat and walked down the steps, intending to intercept him before he got his hopes up.

The sun was at his back and in her eyes as she walked toward the big old oak tree. The blood was gone from the ground where it had soaked into the dirt, but she would never forget that hot night in July.

Shielding her eyes from the sun, she opened her mouth to greet the job seeker. The polite words were already formed in her mind when she realized she'd stopped dead in her tracks.

He was only yards away now, his wide shoulders blocking out the sun. Her hand went to her throat, and she couldn't seem to move.

"Cairn," she whispered, and for a time her heart seemed to stop.

His expression was solemn beneath the black patch covering one eye. And his features were gaunt, as though he'd lost a great deal of weight.

"I heard you were hiring." His voice was low and vibrant and, if she could trust her ears, less than completely confident with regard to his welcome.

"Yes, but only experienced hands need apply, and I require references." She couldn't take her gaze from his face. So familiar and yet, so different. In addition to the patch, he seemed to have changed inside in some major way.

"References, huh?" His mouth slowly relaxed into a smile. "Personal or professional?"

Her heart was full of questions she wanted to ask. But they could wait. "Both."

He gripped her shoulders with his big hands and very gently pulled her closer. "Personal first," he said in a voice that was wonderfully husky. His mouth covered hers gently, his lips caressing and sweet, the tenderness in his kiss saying the things a strong, self-contained man like Cairn never could.

"How's that?" he whispered when at last he lifted his mouth from hers.

"So far so good," she murmured, linking her arms around his neck. She could scarcely believe he was real, even though the feel of his hard body against hers was as solid and thrilling as ever. "Now, about your tractor driving skills."

His eyebrows drew together and the one eye she could see glinted a warning. "What about them?"

"They need work. Lots and lots of work. And no more driving without your seat belt, Murdock. I don't have time to be pulling you out of a brier patch every time I turn around."

Tears were in her eyes now, and on her lashes. His mouth seemed to tremble as he knuckled them away. "Whatever you say boss, although I have to warn you, I'm stone blind in my left eye."

"And the right?"

"Perfect vision."

Her mouth trembled. Without hearing the words, he knew the questions. "Seems I owe that joker who hit me with a rifle butt a vote of thanks. In Captain Frundt's expert opinion, it was that crack on the head that jolted the shrapnel just far enough for him to save one of the optic nerves."

"Oh, Cairn!"

He didn't tell her that neither the doctor nor he had known that until he'd made the decision to have the operation. Nor did he tell her how difficult it had been to leave that mountaintop, thinking he'd be blind in a few days.

"'Course, I think it happened when I fell off the damned tractor, so let's not be too hasty about condemning my driving skills."

As though he could wait no longer, he crushed her against him and buried his face in the warmth of her neck. "God, sweetheart, I've missed you."

His arms were so tight she had trouble drawing enough breath. Or maybe it was the bubble of joy in her chest that affected her breathing. "Promise me you'll never leave us again, no matter what," she managed to whisper fiercely against his throat.

"I couldn't. Not again. I don't have the strength to go through that kind of hell again."

Murdock held her a long time, his emotions raw, his need to feel her against him acute. He'd imagined this moment countless times in the two months since he'd gone under Frundt's knife.

Picturing her face in his mind had kept him sane during the weeks when his eyes had been bandaged and the outcome of the surgery had been in doubt.

If he'd been permanently blind when the bandages had been removed, he would never have come to her. Or so he'd tried to tell himself over and over while he lay all but motionless in an accursed bed in D Ward, swearing at the nurses who bullied him, and threatening dire consequences at Frundt every time he mouthed reassurances.

Reluctantly, but needing to see her beautiful face for real, he drew back. Her eyes were shining, and her mouth was curved into a heart-stopping smile. He had to take a moment to compose himself before he asked gruffly, "So, does that mean I'm hired?"

"Yes! Oh, yes, you idiot. Hired and shanghaied and put under lock and key, if that's what it takes to keep you around this place permanently."

He smoothed her hair, loving the feel of it against his palm. "If that's what you want, it would probably work a lot better if we were married."

She opened her mouth to accept, but found she couldn't force out a word. His laugh was rich and sexy, and his eye was dark with emotion. "Another first. B.J. Berryman, speechless."

"Murdock," she corrected joyfully. "*Mrs*. Cairn Murdock."

*   *   *   *   *

Another wonderful year of romance
concludes with

Christmas Memories

Share in the magic and memories of romance
during the holiday season with this collection of two
full-length contemporary Christmas stories,
by two bestselling authors

**Diana Palmer
Marilyn Pappano**

Available in December at your favorite retail outlet.

MONTANA Mavericks

Stories that capture living and loving
beneath the Big Sky, where legends live
on...and mystery lingers.

This December, explore more MONTANA MAVERICKS with

THE RANCHER TAKES A WIFE
by Jackie Merritt

He'd made up his mind. He'd loved her almost a lifetime
and now he was going to have her, come hell or high
water.

And don't miss a minute of the loving as the passion con-
tinues with:

OUTLAW LOVERS
by Pat Warren (January)

WAY OF THE WOLF
by Rebecca Daniels (February)

THE LAW IS NO LADY
by Helen R. Myers (March)
and many more!

Only from *Silhouette*® where passion lives.

THE BRANIGANS ARE BACK!

You fell in love with the rugged Branigan brood
before—now those brothers have returned...
sexier than ever!

Coming in January from

BRANIGAN'S BREAK by Leslie Davis Guccione

Irresistible Sean Branigan didn't need help raising his
two teenagers—especially from beautiful Julia Hollins!
She was driving him crazy with all her advice...*and*
with her sinfully sexy ways!

Don't miss BRANIGAN'S BREAK (#902) by
Leslie Davis Guccione—only from Silhouette Desire.

HOMETOWN WEDDING
by Pamela Macaluso

Don't miss JUST MARRIED!, a fun-filled new series by Pamela Macaluso about three men with wealth, power and looks to die for. These bad boys had everything—except the love of a good woman.

Bad boy Rorke O'Neil has all the local women's hearts racing. Yet Callie Harrison had learned the hard way just what a wild, worldly hellion Rorke really is...but how can she forget how wonderful it felt to be in his big, strong arms?

Find out in *Hometown Wedding*, coming to you in December...only from

JM